**"Judd, wake up,"** Erin said loudly, shaking him.

He mumbled something she couldn't understand, but show m the deep sleep h of her car. Glaring ny good, since his er feel better. "If y d, "I'll leave you he n the morning twisted like a pretzel."

When her soft threats didn't get any reaction, Erin leaned toward him with the intention of shaking him so hard his teeth would rattle. She never got the chance.

Strong hands clamped around her waist and lifted her over the shift console. She ended up sitting across his muscular thighs, her skirt twisted under her. Pushing against his chest, Erin started to struggle.

"I wouldn't keep moving like that if I were you," he murmured, his voice low and husky with sleep and arousal, his eyes still closed.

"Then let me go."

He opened his eyes. "If that's my only choice, I'd rather you continued wiggling around on my lap. I only thought it was fair to warn you what might happen if you keep rubbing against me like that."

Fighting the sensations caused by Judd's nearness was like trying to stop a tidal wave, and she was just too tired to keep up the battle—especially a battle she didn't particularly want to win. She leaned against him and laid her head on his chest, her breath escaping from her lips in a sigh of pleasure. . . .

## WHAT ARE *LOVESWEPT* ROMANCES?

They are stories of true romance and touching emotion. We believe those two very important ingredients are constants in our highly sensual and very believable stories in the *LOVESWEPT* line. Our goal is to give you, the reader, stories of consistently high quality that may sometimes make you laugh, sometimes make you cry, but are always fresh and creative and contain many delightful surprises within their pages.

Most romance fans read an enormous number of books. Those they truly love, they keep. Others may be traded with friends and soon forgotten. We hope that each *LOVESWEPT* romance will be a treasure—a "keeper." We will always try to publish

*LOVE STORIES YOU'LL NEVER FORGET*
*BY AUTHORS YOU'LL ALWAYS REMEMBER*

The Editors

# Loveswept ® 526

## Patt Bucheister
## Island Lover

**BANTAM BOOKS**
NEW YORK · TORONTO · LONDON · SYDNEY · AUCKLAND

ISLAND LOVER
A Bantam Book / February 1992

If you would be interested in receiving protective vinyl
covers for your Loveswept books, please write to this address
for information:

Loveswept
Bantam Books
P.O. Box 985
Hicksville, NY 11802

ISBN 0-553-44078-0

Published simultaneously in the United States and Canada

PRINTED IN THE UNITED STATES OF AMERICA
OPM     0 9 8 7 6 5 4 3 2 1

# *Prologue*

Judd Stafford slumped down even farther in the upholstered chair opposite his brother-in-law's desk. Sam's old leather chair creaked slightly as Sam leaned forward, resting his forearms on the cluttered top of the desk. He had been studying the various reports in the medical file in front of him for the last four minutes and twenty-two seconds.

Judd was timing him.

Shifting his hips in a vain attempt to find a comfortable position, Judd asked, "Where did you get these chairs, Sam? From some medieval torture chamber?

"Quit your grumbling," Sam answered without glancing up. "Your sister picked out the office furniture. If you have any complaints, take them up with her."

"It's a good thing you aren't an orthopedic surgeon. If your other patients have to sit as long as

I've been here, you'd have to put them back in traction."

Giving his brother-in-law a lopsided grin, Sam let go of the papers he'd been leafing through and sat back. "It's just as well I took Bedside Manner 101 in med school, which emphasized that some patients can try the soul of a saint. I wish I knew what makes every member of your family turn into paranoid horse's butts the minute they walk into this clinic. My staff cringes every time they see any of your family's names in the appointment book."

"The blond X-ray technician didn't seem too upset when she got me on that cold slab. She kept insisting I take all my clothes off."

"From what I've gathered from your sisters," Sam drawled, "most women tend to have that reaction to you."

Judd's smile was pained. "You should know by now not to believe everything my sisters tell you. Your wife brags that you're one of the most brilliant doctors ever to wear a white smock, and I'm still sitting in this poor excuse for a chair, waiting for you to get around to telling me to take two aspirins and to call you in the morning."

Leaning forward in his chair again, Sam tapped Judd's medical file. "Do you want it straight or sugarcoated?"

Judd met his brother-in-law's steady gaze. "What do you think?"

"Straight," Sam murmured. "Of course."

He quickly and efficiently ran over the results of the various tests Judd had taken. After the technical details were out of the way, he added, "Even though I've just told you how good the test results are, I'm going to recommend you take a vacation, Judd. If you have half the sense of a grapefruit, you'll take my advice."

Crossing an ankle over his knee, Judd stared at his highly polished black shoe. "You just went through all that medical jargon to tell me that I'm in good shape. Why do I need a vacation?"

"Judd, you're thirty-two, not twenty-two. You've been working twelve to fourteen hours a day, seven days a week, for years. You came to see me because you've been having trouble sleeping. According to all the tests you've taken, there's no physical reason for your insomnia. That leaves stress and overwork as possible causes. As your doctor, I'm going to prescribe a month of rest and relaxation. As your friend, I hope you'll do as I suggest."

Judd shook his head. "I have too much to do to take time off for a vacation."

"What started out as necessity when you were twenty-four years old has now become a habit. Your mother and your three sisters no longer need your financial support. Stafford Industries is a Fortune 500 company. You've got more money than you'll ever need. When was the last time you did something just for the hell of of it?"

"I made an appointment to see my brother-in-law for a physical. Look how well that's turning out."

Sam ignored Judd's sarcasm. "Now is as good a time as any to take some well-earned time to recharge your batteries. Go to a tropical island, find a scantily clad member of the female species, and forget about business for a while."

Judd levered his long body out of the chair and stood up. "I'll think about it. If I do take time off, the last thing I'll do is go looking for some woman. My mother and sisters are the reason I'll die a happy, contented, crusty old bachelor. Living with them has cured me of wanting to have a woman in my life permanently."

"I didn't say you have to marry the woman, just play with her. You haven't done much playing in years. It's about time you started."

"No, thanks," Judd said succinctly. "I haven't met a woman yet that didn't have her hand out for my money. You have my permission to have me committed if I'm ever insane enough to become seriously involved with a woman."

"Could I have that in writing?"

"I'll have it engraved in stone."

# One

Judd glanced around to see if anyone was observing him as he stood in front of the Stafford Building in downtown Honolulu. Naturally, there weren't as many cars driving by on Kapiolani Boulevard at midnight as there were during the day. A few people were walking along the sidewalk on the opposite side of the street, but no one seemed to be paying any attention to him. As an added precaution, he waited until they were out of sight before digging into his pocket for his keys.

He felt ridiculous sneaking into his own office building like a thief in the night. But, he rationalized, if his sister would answer his questions about a couple of important contract negotiations he'd started before he went on vacation, he wouldn't have to snoop around in the office files in the middle of the night. His name was on the building, the stationery, and the paychecks, and he wasn't supposed to enter his own building for the next two weeks.

Having a brother-in-law as his personal physician had been a big mistake. All Judd had done was go see Sam for a yearly physical, then all hell had broken loose. Judd had planned to ignore Sam's suggestion about taking a vacation, but his brother-in-law had gone home and reported to his wife what his advice to Judd had been. Karen had immediately called her mother and two sisters, which had resulted in the Stafford women ganging up on Judd. On the phone and in person, they'd argued that he hadn't taken any time off since he'd taken over the family business in San Francisco eight years earlier.

Working seven days a week, fourteen hours a day, would take a heavy toll on anyone, they'd lectured, and he wasn't Superman. When that reasoning hadn't made him contact his travel agent, they'd resorted to persistent nagging, with a little guilt thrown in about how many people he would hurt if he didn't take care of his health.

The guilt finally did the trick. His mother and sisters occasionally drove him crazy, especially when they were involved in one of their numerous matchmaking schemes. Still, he couldn't withstand the pressure of knowing they were seriously worried about him. No matter how much he assured them he was only a little tired, they didn't believe him.

Eventually they wore him down, and he compromised by agreeing to take two weeks off instead of a month.

The threat his mother made about coming to stay with him to make sure he was taking care of himself might have had something to do with his decision too.

For the past three days he'd been staying in his company's condominium in Honolulu instead of residing in his high-rise apartment in San Francisco. From the glimpses he'd had of some of his attractive neighbors, there were possibilities of female companionship if he wanted it. The condo had all the comforts of a first-class hotel, including a king-size bed and a view that was picture-postcard perfect. Unfortunately, he wasn't getting any more sleep there than he had in his own bed in San Francisco.

What he was doing was slowly going nuts from boredom. There was only so much sun, sea, and fresh air a man could take, especially one accustomed to the exciting thrust and parry of the business world. From what Judd could tell so far, vacations were highly overrated.

After glancing around the street one more time, he used the appropriate key to turn off the alarm system before opening the heavy glass door to the Stafford Building. He'd timed his arrival to coincide with the rounds the security guard made at midnight. It was probably too much to ask of fate that he could be in the building without the guard's knowledge, but he would just as soon the guard didn't know how long he was there. If he did get caught, he would simply explain who he was—and hope the guard didn't call his sister.

Judd scowled as he remembered Justine telling

him she'd instructed the security guards who manned the desk in the lobby to report to her if he so much as set one foot inside the building. The same tenacity that made Justine a good vice president in charge of operations of the branch office in Hawaii, also made her a tough opponent when it came to protecting her family. Even when a certain family member didn't think he needed that protection.

Judd had to admit his long days were beginning to tell on him physically and mentally. There had been occasions lately, at the end of a typically hectic day, when he felt much older than thirty-two. Even after the pressure of pulling Stafford Industries back from the edge of disaster that his father had driven it to had eased, he hadn't relaxed his busy schedule. One of the reasons he'd never taken time off before was he'd never found anything as exciting, as interesting, as challenging as working.

Which was why he was sneaking into his own building at midnight. Since he couldn't sleep, he'd taken a walk and ended up in front of the Stafford Building. Since he was there, he'd decided to see what progress Justine had made on the Kasagi contract.

He closed the door behind him, then reset the alarm system and started walking toward the bank of elevators. The unexpected sound of a woman singing slightly off-key stopped him in his tracks. He turned his head in the direction of the singing. A woman was standing in front of the east wall of the lobby, her arm raised as she applied paint to a half-finished mural. For a moment, he wondered if he was in the right building. Feeling like an idiot, he looked around and saw *Stafford Industries* in bold gold lettering on the wall facing the front entrance. He was in the right place.

He turned his head to stare again at the woman surrounded by painting paraphernalia. He removed his glasses, rubbed his eyes, then replaced them. Phew, he thought with relief. She wasn't a figment of his imagination. It was comforting to know he hadn't lost his mind. Lack of sleep could do funny things to a person's system, but he hadn't started seeing things. Justine's refusal to discuss anything about the business apparently included neglecting to inform him that she had arranged to have a mural painted in the lobby.

Judd continued to stare, intrigued by the sight of the black-haired woman standing on a large dropcloth that covered the floor, her slim figure highlighted by several floodlights that illuminated her and the mural.

Her slender hips and her ponytail swayed back and forth as she kept time to the music only she could hear through the transistor headset covering her ears. The song was apparently a lively tune, since she was moving at a quick pace, and the way she was gyrating was doing invigorating things to his system.

His gaze was drawn from her undulating hips to her bare legs, exposed by the mid-thigh–length denim skirt she wore. After appreciating her shapely legs, he let his gaze roam upward. Her cotton sweater was a soft orange shade, the sleeves pushed up to her elbows, the ribbed hem barely reaching her waist. Several wooden bangle bracelets clattered softly with the movements of her right hand as she stroked paint on the mural, then lowered her hand to the palette sitting on a high stool next to her.

Dragging his gaze away from her, he looked at the painting. It was a tropical scene of palm trees, sandy beaches, and a series of grass huts from an earlier period of Hawaiian history. He saw several figures outlined in white against the blue sky and lush green foliage that hadn't been fleshed out with paint yet. From what he could see of the work already completed, which was almost half of the entire wall, the woman—if she'd done all the artwork—was very talented.

Curiosity overcame his original intention of checking on the Kasagi contract, and he walked toward the artist. He stopped several feet away and watched her, amused by her enthusiastic singing as she applied a dark green paint to palm fronds. He didn't have to hear the music to be aware that it had changed to a slower rhythm. Her lower body rolled and swayed in a provocative motion that made his blood thicken and his heart rate accelerate.

He hadn't even had a glimpse of her face, and his hormones were kicking in, he thought with astonishment. Lack of sleep might have slowed his reflexes a little, but it certainly hadn't affected other bodily functions.

Unable to wait any longer to see what she looked like from the front, he walked right up to her while her attention was in the other direction as she loaded more paint on her brush. He waited for her to turn back to the mural, and was aware of the moment she realized she had company.

She met his eyes without any sign of fear or surprise, making him wonder if she was accustomed to midnight interruptions. She pushed the headphones down until they circled her neck and said calmly, "Hi."

"Hi," he replied automatically, staring down at her.

Her eyes were a deep blue, like the color of the sky just before the sun disappeared at the end of a stormy day. Her long lashes were as black as her hair, making him think of a description his Irish grandmother had once made about his young niece's blue eyes having been put in with a sooty finger. Her skin was lightly tanned, and her lips were sensually shaped and inviting, even though she wasn't smiling.

He felt a sudden urge to find out how she tasted, to feel her mouth under his. Or to see her smile. He would settle for the smile for now.

She accepted his thorough examination without any obvious sign of self-consciousness, her clear gaze appraising him at the same time. He found himself wondering if she approved of what she saw as much as he approved of her. He usually took his own looks for granted, so this particular insecurity surprised him.

So did his reaction to her.

He reached up and removed his glasses, not

because he wanted to give her a clearer view of his eyes, but in order to see her better.

He smiled. "When I was little, my grandmother used to tell me stories of the elves that came out at night in Ireland to paint the landscape so it would be green and beautiful every morning. I always thought it was just one of her Irish fairy tales. Until now."

He saw surprise flicker in her stunning eyes and waited. When she smiled, he had to clench his hands to keep from touching her mouth.

"I could use a wee bit of help from the little people about now," she said in a thick Irish brogue. "It's too bad this isn't Ireland."

Copying her, he also used an Irish accent. "They won't come out if anyone's around, you know. They turn to stone if anyone sees them."

"That's leprechauns," she said, dropping the accent, "not elves."

He grinned. "So it is. Would I be correct in assuming you have an Irish grandmother, too?"

"Grandfather. He used to blame the leprechauns for misplacing whatever it was he couldn't find. The more absentminded he became, the more he claimed the leprechauns were bedeviling him."

"Did he tell you about the pot of gold at the end of the rainbow?"

She nodded. "Every time it rained. I even went looking for the end of a rainbow a couple of times."

He slid his glance to the mural. She was standing at the base of the rainbow she'd painted on the wall. "I never believed that either, until now."

She turned to see what he was looking at, then

glanced back at him. "First an elf, now a pot of gold. The blarney is flowing thick and fast tonight."

He was tempted to warn her that she hadn't heard anything yet, but he changed the subject instead. "I suppose you hear it all the time, but your work is very good."

She smiled, although somewhat guardedly. "I don't know of any artist who gets tired of hearing someone compliment his or her work." She stepped back several paces to give herself a wider view of the mural. "It's gradually coming together. No matter how many I've done, I'm always apprehensive about the finished product living up to my original concept."

He backed up to stand beside her, allowing himself the same perspective she had. Replacing his glasses, he scanned the area she'd been working on. "Do you always work this late at night?"

"When it's necessary. It depends on the location. This building has a great deal of foot traffic during the day, so I arranged to have access to the lobby after the building is closed to the public. I've tried to work in public buildings during regular hours. Fending off little boys with ice cream cones, advice from amateur painters, and answering continuous questions about my technique doesn't make for an ideal work environment."

"Not to mention the men who must have tried to hit on you."

She met his gaze. "Is that what you're trying to do?"

Judd saw no reason to hide his interest in her. "I

haven't quite made up my mind what I'm going to do about you."

"Until you do, why don't you tell me what you're doing here?"

"Would you believe I'm part of the cleaning crew?"

Her gaze traveled over his light tan shirt and spotless white slacks, and she shook her head. "During the two weeks I've been working here, I've met everyone on the cleaning crew. Besides, they come on Tuesdays and Thursdays. This is Wednesday. Try again."

"How about a cat burglar?"

"Unless you have a fetish for office equipment, there isn't much worth stealing. This is a business office, not a jewelry store. The security guard is making his rounds at the moment, so he couldn't have let you in. That means you must have a key or the alarm would have gone off. And that means you apparently work for Stafford Industries."

He could have corrected her by saying he *was* Stafford Industries, but for some reason he didn't feel like telling her who he was just yet.

"You sure you're an artist?" he asked. "You'd make a great detective."

"I think it's called common sense," she said dryly.

She walked away from him, stopping near a canvas satchel lying on the dropcloth. Reaching inside, she withdrew a fat red thermos and a plastic cup. She poured coffee into the cup, then held it out to him. "Would you like some?"

He shook his head. "No, thanks. The last thing I

need at this hour is caffeine. I don't need any help staying awake."

Whether she heard the wry note in his voice or was unusually perceptive, she tilted her head to one side and asked, "Having a little trouble sleeping?"

He shrugged, hating to admit to what he considered a weakness. He'd always been able to control every aspect of his life until these bouts of insomnia. He caught the smile curving her lips.

"What?" he asked.

"You remind me of my brother. When Sean broke his arm playing softball, he insisted on finishing the game with his arm tucked into his shirt, rather than give in and go to the hospital. He wouldn't concede he was a mere human being with a temporary problem either."

Judd smiled faintly, acknowledging her point. "It's not as easy to be macho as you women seem to think it is."

"Apparently not." After taking a sip of coffee, she said pointedly, "Bert is going to be back any minute. He's the security guard. If you aren't supposed to be here, you might think about ducking into a broom closet or something."

Earlier he might have tried to stay out of the security guard's way, but not now. "I'll take care of the guard."

"I hope you don't mean that literally. Bert has five children and a sweet wife who adores him. I don't imagine they would appreciate you harming him in any way."

"If he has all those kids, he probably won't mind

having his palms greased. I've found cold cash usually opens a lot of doors."

She considered that for a moment. "A cynical insomniac," was her only comment.

"I'm not cynical. Just realistic. Everyone has a price. You can relax, though. I won't have to resort to bribery in this case. I have a legitimate reason for being here."

Her gaze remained on his face a few seconds longer, and he was waiting for her to ask him what the reasons were. He was a little put out when she didn't. Instead she pursed her lips, as if in thought, and he felt an overwhelming desire to kiss that pouting look shaping her mouth.

She intrigued him. And attracted him. None of her reactions to him were what he expected, and he liked the challenge of keeping up with her. It certainly beat staring at the walls of the condo.

"Who are you?" he asked suddenly, needing to put a name to this strangely fascinating woman.

She didn't answer him right away. She studied him as though weighing the option of answering or ignoring his question, then finally spoke.

"I'm Erin."

"Erin," he repeated slowly. He didn't push for a last name, but she supplied it anyway.

"Erin Callahan."

"A nice Irish name. You're an unusual woman, Erin Callahan."

She raised one brow. "No one's ever thought so before. Haven't you ever seen an artist?"

"Not like you."

He could tell from her expressive eyes that she

wasn't sure whether he'd just given her a compliment or not. After staring back at him for a few seconds, she said, "When the police ask me for information for their police report, it would help if I could give them your name."

He smiled, amused by her roundabout way of asking him who he was. "I'm Judd. Actually, it's Judson, but I only use that on my driver's license and my passport or any other document where they get cranky if you use a shortened version of your name."

"Judd is your first name?"

"Yes."

"You don't have a last name?"

"I have one. You just don't need to know what it is yet."

"Why? Is it on a wanted poster somewhere?"

"Not that I know of."

"Well, Judd, it's been interesting chatting with you, but I need to get back to work."

Without waiting for him to comment, she turned away and returned to the stool that held her paints and brushes. He couldn't help being pleased that she didn't put the headset back on. She wasn't going to shut herself off from him and pretend he wasn't there.

"Does it bother you if someone watches you work, Erin?"

She shrugged. "It depends on why they want to watch. Are you interested in painting or just bored?"

He was experiencing a variety of sensations, but

boredom wasn't one of them. "I'm more interested in the artist than the artwork."

"Ah," she murmured. "You're bored."

Before he could contradict her, he heard a pinging sound indicating an elevator had arrived on the ground floor. It was followed shortly by the unmistakable sound of hard leather soles on marble floor. Judd didn't turn to see if the security guard had reached his desk yet. His gaze remained on Erin.

She paused in the act of mixing paints and looked at him, a frankly curious expression in her eyes as she waited to see what he would do.

The footsteps were coming nearer. Judd smiled at her. "I'll be back," he said, then turned away to have a little chat with the security guard.

Erin dragged her attention back to the palette, telling herself to concentrate on that rather than how Bert was going to deal with the smooth-talking stranger. The security guard was getting paid to check out people in the building. She was getting paid to paint.

She hadn't been all that surprised to see someone in the building at that hour. One of the things she'd discovered since she started working at night was that a number of people preferred darkness to daylight. Their reasons were as varied as the people themselves. Most of the people she'd met were involved in doing their own work, like the cleaning crew and security guards.

Judd might have been an intriguing interruption, but she wasn't interested in following up on the attraction she'd felt spring up between them. The last thing she wanted was to become attracted to a man when she'd only recently acquired her independence from her overprotective brothers. She was finally able to move without having one of them looking over her shoulder to make sure she wasn't going to bump into anything that might hurt her. It had taken her a long time to convince them she was capable of taking care of herself, and she was reveling in the freedom.

Refusing to satisfy her curiosity to see how the stranger was faring with Bert, she concentrated on mixing lemon yellow with a touch of black to create a soft green color for the palm fronds. Then she pressed the palette knife into a little Prussian blue and added it to the green, changing the color to a deeper shade. She spread the paint out a little over the palette and studied it. She frowned. She'd unconsciously mixed the deep green color of Judd's eyes.

She scraped the paint onto the knife, then wiped it off on a paper towel so she wouldn't have to look at it.

Irritated with herself, she proceeded to mix the color she needed. She usually worked from seven in the evening until two in the morning, with a set amount of the mural to complete each day. There were still a couple of hours left before she could quit, and her time would be better used if she concentrated on the mural instead of the tall, mysterious man who'd appeared from nowhere.

She felt an odd prickling sensation on the back

of her neck and turned her head to look over her shoulder. Judd was half sitting on the guard's desk, his arms casually folded across his chest as he listened to what Bert was saying. He was staring at her.

Tearing her gaze away from him, she glanced at Bert to see what his reaction was to the intruder. Resembling a short version of Santa Claus minus the beard, and wearing a khaki uniform instead of a white-trimmed red coat, Bert was standing in front of the stranger. And he was smiling.

Jerking her attention back to the mural, Erin adjusted the headphones until they were covering her ears and the music blocked out any other sounds. She poised her brush over the area she was determined to complete that night.

Unable to resist one last look, she glanced over her shoulder again and saw that Bert was sitting behind the desk reading a newspaper. He was alone. She tamped down the disappointment she felt. She should be relieved, she told herself, that Judd was gone, but she couldn't help wondering why he'd been in the building in the first place. Or why her heart had started beating like a snare drum in a marching band.

After a few minutes of concentrated effort, she managed to shut out the world around her and lose herself in her painting.

She'd completed all the palm fronds and had moved on to the roof of a grass shack when she sensed someone was beside her. Jerking her head around, she caught her breath as she stared into Judd's amused green eyes.

With her free hand, she tugged the headset down. "How much did it cost you?"

He blinked. "For what?"

"To pay off the security guard."

"Not a cent. My charming personality was enough." His smile broadened when her mouth twisted in a skeptical grimace. He raised his right hand. "I swear it's the truth."

Reverting to the Irish accent again, she drawled, "I know better than to believe the words of a man with blarney in his veins."

"Would it help if I told you the Irish blood has been watered down considerably by a Scottish grandfather and an English mother?"

"Not a lot."

He placed his hand on his heart as though she'd wounded him. "I can see I have my work cut out for me to convince you I'm not feeding you a line."

"Speaking of work, don't you have any to do? Or is bothering people your life's work?"

"I'm on vacation. Bothering people is just a sideline."

"Well, I'm not on vacation. If I expect to get paid, I need to work on this mural."

"I've recently been given some good advice about how a person can work too much. Maybe you would like to hear it."

"No, thank you. I'm sure I've heard just about every variation of the same theme."

He held up a carry-out bag from one of the restaurants in the Ala Moana Shopping Center. "Bert mentioned that you hadn't taken a break since seven o'clock. He recommended a Chinese restaurant nearby, so I picked up some food. There's plenty left, even after Bert got his share."

Erin glanced in Bert's direction, but the security guard didn't notice. He was occupied with a pair of chopsticks and a white take-out carton.

"I see Bert can be bought after all," she murmured, bringing her attention back to Judd.

Judd walked over to a nearby marble bench and set the bag down on it. Looking back at her, he asked, "Are you going to make me eat all this by myself?"

A delicious aroma of spices and fragrant sauces was undermining her willpower. "I'm afraid so. I really need to finish this section if I'm going to stay on schedule."

Judd sat and leaned back against the wall, stretching his long legs out in front of him as he unwrapped an egg roll. His eyelids were getting heavy, one of the familiar signs of exhaustion. There was also burning eyes, the sapped strength in his muscles, the muted buzzing in his ears, as though his head were underwater. What wasn't familiar was the strange contentment that came over him when he was with Erin Callahan. He doubted if she would be very flattered with that announcement. She might think it made her sound like a pair of old felt slippers. For now, he didn't want to tell her anything, though. All he wanted to do was listen.

"Can you talk and paint at the same time?" he asked.

She shrugged. "It depends on what you want to

talk about. If it's Einstein's theory of relativity, you're on your own."

He wanted her to talk about herself, but he settled for a topic he felt she would be more comfortable with. Surveying the mural, he asked, "How long does a project like this usually take?"

Erin glanced at him over her shoulder. Once again, he hadn't moved in the direction she'd expected him to take. For now, she'd go along for the ride.

"From start to finish," she said, "a mural this size with a fairly simple subject takes a little more than a month. A week to sketch the panel in scale, another week to transfer the drawing onto the wall, then two or three weeks to paint it."

"If a company wants to hire you to paint a mural, how do they go about contacting you?"

"We're in the phone book."

"We?"

"I'm part of a group of artists who've joined together in a co-op. We share the expenses of running a gallery and workshop called Hale Hana."

"Hale Hana?"

"It means workshop."

"How many are in your group?"

"Five," she answered, wondering if he was just making conversation or if he really wanted to know. Giving him the benefit of the doubt, she went on. "We went to art school together, and all any of us wanted to do when we graduated was paint. Alone we didn't think we stood much chance of surviving, so we combined our talents and our meager finances and formed Hale Hana.

Most of our commissions so far come from word-of-mouth recommendations."

"Is that how Stafford Industries found you?"

Hearing a drowsy note in his voice, she glanced over at him. He was lazily watching her as he leaned back against the wall, and he wasn't even pretending to eat any of the food he'd brought back with him.

If he were any more relaxed, she thought with envy, he'd be asleep.

Continuing her work, she stroked some paint on the wall as she answered his question. "The woman who hired me to do this mural came out to Hale Hana one weekend when we were having an exhibit. She bought one of my paintings and asked to see my portfolio. A month or so later, she called and asked me to come to the Stafford Building to see the wall she wanted decorated in the lobby. I gave Mrs. Garrison a cost estimate and later a series of preliminary sketches. She approved them after making a few suggestions of her own."

"That sounds like Justine. She's always put her two cents' worth in whether she could afford it or not."

His voice was so low, Erin could barely hear him. She turned to look at him once more. The first thing she noticed was that he had taken off his glasses and was holding them in his hand, which was resting on his thigh. The second was that his eyes were closed. His chest rose and fell slowly.

He was asleep.

# Two

What a strange night, Erin thought as she nibbled on the end of her paintbrush. What a strange man. From the cut of Judd's clothes and the expensive gold watch he wore, she surmised he could afford any room in any hotel in Waikiki. With his casual arrogance and his attractive looks, he wouldn't have any difficulty finding a beautiful woman to spend the evening with at any of the numerous nightclubs in Waikiki or Honolulu.

During their brief acquaintance, he'd impressed her as a man who would have doors open to him wherever he went. For some reason, he'd opened the door of the Stafford Building and walked in.

So why was she feeling sorry for him? she wondered abstractedly. Just because the man chose to sleep on a hard bench instead of in a soft bed might make him a bit eccentric, but not the object of sympathy. Still, the feeling was there.

Bert's usual rumbling voice was a gravelly whisper as he spoke just behind her. "I was telling Marjory just this morning that nothing ever happens here at night. Wait until she hears about this. I have instructions to call Mrs. Garrison if her brother comes to the building, but Mr. Stafford said he'd tell her he was here himself."

Erin slowly turned to look at the security guard. "Mr. Stafford?" She pointed to the lettering on the wall. "*That* Mr. Stafford?"

Bert nodded, his gaze on the sleeping man. "The man himself. I thought he'd be older, more stuffy, you know? He was joking with me just like a regular guy. When Mrs. Garrison told me to report to her if he came to the building, I thought maybe he was half off his nut or something. He seems like an all right guy to me, so I'm not calling her. Besides, he reminded me I should do as he says 'cause he's the boss."

Looking back at Judd Stafford, Erin frowned. He'd had a chance to tell her who he was when she'd asked his name, but he hadn't. Obviously, he had his reasons, just as he must have his reasons for coming to the building in the middle of the night. Whatever they were, they didn't have anything to do with her.

Keeping her voice low, she asked. "Do you know where Mr. Stafford is staying, Bert?"

"Yeah. In the company condo a couple of blocks from here. I guess I'd better call a cab. He can't very well spend the rest of the night where he is. Do you think he might be sick or something?"

Erin remembered his remark about not having

trouble staying awake when she'd offered him coffee earlier. "I think he's just tired." She glanced at her watch. It was almost two o'clock. "I might as well leave now too."

"Could you wait until the cab gets here before you leave? I can walk you to your car after I get Mr. Stafford on his way."

"You don't need to escort me to my car tonight, Bert. I'll be all right. I'm not parked that far away."

"I promised your brother I would see that you didn't walk to your car alone at this hour of the night." Bert slapped his forehead when he saw her eyes widen in surprise. "Me and my big mouth. He told me not to tell you he'd been checking up on you."

Even though she thought she already knew the answer, she asked, "Which one of my brothers talked to you?"

The guard frowned as he struggled to remember. Then his eyes brightened. "Michael. Michael Callahan. I have his phone number somewhere in my desk. He asked me to call him if you have any problems."

Even from Maui her brother kept tabs on her. "When did you talk to him?"

"He called here that first night you were setting up your equipment. He seemed real concerned about your welfare, which I thought was nice. Families should watch out for each other. I told him I'd take care of you as though you were my own daughter."

This seemed to be the night for revelations of one sort or another, Erin decided. "I appreciate

you looking out for me since I've been here, Bert,"
she said quietly, knowing the older man meant
what he said. It wasn't his fault her brother still
thought of her as a child who shouldn't cross a
street alone.

Bert scratched his head as he glanced at Judd. "I
guess I'd better get on the horn to get a cab for Mr.
Stafford. We might as well let him sleep until it gets
here."

After Bert returned to his desk to make the
phone call, Erin cleaned her brushes and placed
her palette and other painting equipment in the
small wooden trunk her brother Sean had built for
her. The she positioned barriers across the area
she'd been working on, setting the stainless steel
posts and thick velvet ropes so that they would
keep people at a safe distance from the wall.

When there was nothing left for her to do, she
approached Judd, who was still sleeping. Crouch-
ing down, she gently took his glasses from his
hand, folded them, and stuck them into his shirt
pocket. Then she touched his knee.

"Mr. Stafford?" she said softly. When he showed
no signs of hearing her, she tried again, shaking
his leg slightly. "Mr. Stafford. Judd. Wake up."

He slowly opened his eyes. "Erin?"

The low drowsy growl of his voice sent shivers
down her spine. "Yes. Bert's calling you a cab to
take you to your condo. It should be here in a few
minutes."

His fingers closed over her hand that was still on
his knee. "How long have I been asleep?"

"Not long. Maybe thirty minutes."

A corner of his mouth curved upward in a rueful smile. "I usually don't fall asleep when I'm with a beautiful woman. You have a soothing voice."

"Now there's a compliment a woman doesn't hear often enough," Erin drawled. "It makes me sound like a tranquilizer. Or deadly boring."

"I meant it as a compliment." He laced his fingers through hers and wouldn't let her pull her hand away when she tried. "However," he said, sliding their joined hands farther up his thigh, "the effect you have on some parts of me isn't as relaxing as others."

"You need more sleep," she said dryly. "You're hallucinating."

His thumb stroked the back of her hand. "I don't suppose you'd consider coming back to my apartment? If you were with me, I'd stand a better chance of catching up on my sleep. I don't understand why that is, but I'm desperate enough to try anything that works."

Her heartbeat had accelerated when he'd linked his fingers with hers. Now her breath caught in her chest at his suggestion. Refusing to take him seriously, she tugged her hand out of his hold and straightened up.

"I haven't had such a flattering offer since I was in high school and the captain of the football team asked me to go to the senior prom because I was the right height to be his dancing partner. I'll pass on your offer, Mr. Stafford."

His eyes searched hers thoroughly after she spoke his name. "You know who I am."

"Bert didn't realize I wasn't supposed to know."

Judd was going to explain why he hadn't told her, but Bert chose that moment to rejoin them. "A taxi just pulled up out front, Mr. Stafford," he said.

Judd's gaze never left Erin's face as he acknowledged Bert's announcement. "Thanks. I'll be there in a minute."

The security guard looked from Erin to Judd, then back to Erin. "Let me know when you're ready to leave, Miss Callahan, and I'll walk you to your car."

Judd stood up. "I'll escort Erin to her car, Bert."

Erin didn't even try to protest, knowing it wouldn't do any good. Bert would do as he was told by the man who owned the company that paid his salary. She walked over to her canvas satchel and picked it up. Giving the area a last-minute check to make sure she hadn't forgotten anything, she adjusted one of the signs hanging from the barrier that warned of wet paint, then began to walk toward the entrance.

Judd fell into step beside her, taking the satchel from her. When they reached the door, he deactivated the alarm before unlocking the door. After she exited the building, Erin waited while he reversed the procedure. The cool night air blew around her, refreshing her after the long hours in the enclosed lobby.

"Where's your car?" he asked as he took her arm.

She gestured toward the parking lot next to the building. His building, she reminded herself. Knowing he was the wealthy owner of Stafford Industries didn't intimidate her, but the fact that he hadn't told her earlier puzzled her. He could have used that information in an attempt to impress her, but he hadn't. Of course, she admitted wryly, he didn't need to try to impress her. She found him attractive enough as it was.

He drew her along with him to the taxi parked at the curb, its motor running. Judd leaned down to tell the driver to wait for him, then they headed for her car.

As he shortened his long stride to accommodate hers, he asked, "Do you have very far to drive home?"

"It depends on what you consider far. I live in Haleiwa. At this time of the morning, there isn't much traffic, so it takes me about thirty minutes."

"Do you live alone?"

"No."

He stopped walking abruptly and turned her around to face him. "Damn," he muttered. "You aren't wearing a ring."

"I'm not married," she said patiently.

"Why won't he marry you?"

"Who?"

"The man you live with."

"Actually, I live with two men."

His head jerked back as though she'd just slapped him. *"What?"*

She chuckled, enjoying his shocked reaction. "Also two women."

"You live with four people?"

"You make it sound indecent. Two of my housemates are married to each other and the other two are just friends."

After a brief pause, he said, "I thought the sixties communes were dead."

"Poverty isn't. We all live together because it's cheaper than living separately, and the cottage is next to the gallery." She reached over to take her satchel from his hand. Pointing to the minivan parked about ten feet away, she added, "I can go alone the rest of the way. Your meter is running, Mr. Stafford."

He stopped her from walking away from him by clasping his hand around her wrist. "Do me a big favor, Erin. Drop the 'Mr. Stafford.' Don't try to use who I am to keep me at a distance. It won't work."

Tightening her grip on her satchel, she lifted her chin and looked directly into his eyes. "Then how about if I point out that you are going to be on the island for only a short time? There are plenty of attractive women here who are more than happy to entertain tourists during their stays. I'm not one of them. Take my word for it. I am not interested in being your entertainment while you're on vacation."

His eyes narrowed as he looked down at her. His voice was dangerously low as he murmured. "I don't think I can take your word for it. I need to find out for myself whether you're interested or not."

As he lowered his head toward her, she opened her mouth to protest, but she wasn't given a chance to say anything. Taking advantage of her parted lips, Judd covered her mouth with his. She couldn't hold back a soft sound of pleasure as he cupped the back of her head and deepened the kiss. Her skin heated with a sensual fire that the evening breeze could not cool. Her heart felt as though it had stopped beating, then it thudded heavily when his arm slipped around her waist and brought her firmly against his hard body. His scent and his taste overwhelmed her, making her forget everything but him.

Her response frightened her. Physical attraction she could accept and deal with. But not this devastating need.

She pushed him away, needing to put some distance between them. When her gaze fell to her hands pressing against his solid chest, she was startled to discover she must have dropped her satchel during those tumultuous minutes. Feeling as though she were moving in slow motion, she bent down to pick up the satchel, then straightened.

She started walking toward her minivan without saying a single word to Judd. She didn't trust herself to look at him, or even to say good night.

Judd didn't try to stop her. Stunned by what had happened between them, he remained where he was while she started the engine, put the van in gear, and drove out of the parking lot. He watched the red taillights become smaller and smaller, then finally disappear. Still, he didn't move. What had started out as a test to determine whether Erin was as disinterested in him as she claimed, had turned into something altogether different from anything he'd ever experienced before.

He'd gotten his answer, but now he had a few more questions.

The sound of a horn honking jolted him from his thoughts, and he turned around to walk back to the waiting taxi. He had a feeling he'd had all the sleep he was going to get that night.

Erin was a half hour late arriving at the Stafford Building the following night. It seemed like she'd been behind schedule from the moment her alarm had jarred her awake. Her day probably would have been easier to get through if she could have kept her mind on what she was doing instead of thinking about Judd Stafford. Or if she had gotten more than just a couple of hours of sleep. Of if she could have forgotten the feel of his mouth covering hers.

Usually she didn't have any trouble sleeping. Working at the gallery and painting during the day and working on the mural at night normally tired her out so much, she fell asleep the moment her head hit the pillow.

But yesterday hadn't been a normal day.

After Bert let her into the building, she set out her supplies automatically, not having to give much thought to what she was doing. Unfortunately, that allowed other thoughts to pop into her mind. Like wondering whether or not Judd Stafford had found someone else to amuse himself with for the evening. It shouldn't matter, she told herself. She'd only spent a few hours with him. There was no reason she should expect to see him again. Or want to see him again. She shouldn't be disappointed he hadn't returned, but she couldn't think of any other word for the letdown feeling that had come over her the minute she'd entered the lobby and found Bert was the only one there.

As she began to mix paint, she dragged her thoughts away from Judd Stafford, thinking instead about the announcement Polly had made that morning. Everyone had been together in the kitchen prior to starting work, and Polly had taken advantage of the opportunity to tell them she was leaving the island that morning. She realized her departure was going to cause a problem for them, what with their rent being due in another week, and she was sorry, but she was leaving the island with the man she'd been dating for the past two weeks.

With the bluntness only longtime friends could get away with, both Wayne and Roy told Polly she was crazy to be taking off with some guy she'd know for such a short time. Erin and Kate were more tactful when they suggested Polly give the relationship more time, but Polly was adamant. She was in love. She couldn't live without him. It wasn't infatuation. This was the real thing, she stated. Even though the four other housemates thought she was making a giant mistake, there wasn't anything they could do about Polly's leaving.

Now Erin had to find someone else to help pay the rent, which wasn't going to be easy. Not many people would be willing to live in a cottage with four other people and share the expenses of rent and upkeep of the Hale Hana Gallery. Add to that the fact that Wayne was a born-again slob and Kate collected wind chimes. Then there was Roy, who had taken over the kitchen and insisted everyone eat the healthy meals he made with tofu and seaweed.

Finding another renter who was also an artist was going to be even more difficult. Polly's seascapes had sold well and had contributed considerably to the gallery coffers. Only by sharing expenses could they all manage to keep the gallery going and have a little left over. Hale Hana was just beginning to show a profit, and the loss of Polly was going to create quite a hardship unless they found someone to replace her immediately. The rent was due in less than a week.

The lease was in Erin's name, the total amount of the rent was her responsibility. She hated to give Michael or her other brothers the satisfaction of saying she couldn't make it on her own. Somehow she would find the money.

Erin was painting the lavalava on one of the male figures when she became aware of the low mumble of voices behind her. Her fingers tightened on the paintbrush when she recognized both voices. Bert's raspy low rumble she had heard often during her long evenings in the building. The other resonant male tone she'd only heard once before, but would never forget.

Slowly, cautiously, she looked over her shoulder in the direction of Bert's desk. The security guard was leaning back in his chair, the two front legs off the floor as he looked up at the tall man perched on a corner of the desk. As on the previous night, Judd's hair had been slightly mussed by the wind, but snug jeans and a white cotton sweater, the sleeves pushed up to his elbows, replaced the stylishly casual clothing he'd worn before. His forearms appeared to be darker, matching the tanned skin of his face. Apparently he'd been enjoying some of the island's beaches during the day.

When he shifted his attention from Bert to her, he caught her gaze and held it. Whether for his benefit or her own, Erin shook her head slightly, as though refusing whatever it was his eyes demanded from her.

Feeling as wary as a defenseless doe being pursued by a relentless hunter, she broke away from his intense gaze. Even though she couldn't hide her reaction from herself, she thought as she lifted her brush, the least she could do was hide it from him.

She sensed he was near her before she actually saw him. The air around her suddenly seemed charged with electricity, and an awareness skidded along her veins. Lifting her chin defensively, she turned her head and met the frank appraisal in his green eyes.

"Out walking the streets again, Mr. Stafford?"

"I thought we'd already decided to get rid of the formal use of my last name."

"Did we? I must have missed that," she said coolly.

The amused glint in his eyes implied he knew exactly what she was doing, and that she wasn't going to get away with it.

"I tried to call you today at the gallery."

She wasn't able to hide her surprise this time. "Why?"

"Come on, Erin. You're an intelligent woman. You know why."

She stopped all pretense of trying to work and faced him. "All I know is that you're apparently at loose ends, and you seem to expect me to tie them up for you."

"Sounds kinky, but that's not exactly what I had in mind. I was thinking more of getting to know an interesting, attractive woman. As far as I know, the custom of a man and a woman sharing a meal, some conversation, and a bed isn't unheard of here."

"Sharing a meal is out of the question under the circumstances."

"You don't eat?"

"Usually on the run. My schedule is a little full at the moment."

"All right," he said, his gaze holding hers. "You've eliminated going out for dinner, or in your case, breakfast. We've already shared a conversation. What about sharing a bed?"

While she refused to take him seriously, she was having difficulty blocking out visions of being in his arms, pressed against his firm naked flesh.

"Maybe they do things a bit quicker in San Francisco than we do here," she said, "but I don't know a single woman who hops into bed after spending a couple of hours with a man in the lobby of a commercial building."

He folded his arms across his chest, the gesture more contemplative than confrontational. "There was also the kiss we shared in the parking lot in the wee hours of the morning. Have you forgotten that?"

She would find it easier to forget her own name than the way his mouth had felt on hers, she admitted silently. Using the only excuse she had, she looked away from him to wipe off her brush on a rag. "You'll make it easier on both of us if you just take no for an answer, Judd." She held up the brush. "I have work to do."

"I don't plan on taking the easy way. No challenge." He nodded in the direction of the mural. "Go ahead and paint. I'll just sit over here and watch for a while. When you're ready to take a break, we'll discuss how much rent you're asking for the vacant room in your beach house."

Her mouth dropped open and the long-handled paintbrush fell out of her hand, landing on the drop cloth. Closing her mouth with a snap, she simply stared at him. Then she finally managed to say, "Now I know why you're on vacation. You've had a nervous breakdown."

His laughter bounced off the walls. He took off his glasses and grinned at her. "That's what I like about you, Erin. I can always rely on you to speak your mind without any sugarcoating."

Instead of mollifying her, his backhanded compliment triggered her temper. "Oh, I can speak much more plainly than that, Mr. Stafford. You're a certifiable loony."

"I'm not crazy. Bert mentioned you had asked him if he knew of anyone interested in renting a room. I'm applying for the vacancy. I'll pay a full month's rent even though I'll only be staying two weeks. You have to admit that's a good deal."

"You've got to be kidding. What makes you think I would even consider renting the room to you? You own this building and a condo in Honolulu. Your sister, Mrs. Garrison, would undoubtedly put you up at her house if you asked, yet you expect me to believe you need a room in a house full of artists?"

There was no amusement in his eyes now. "I think that's exactly what I need."

Her anger evaporated like smoke. He was serious, she realized. Remembering how she'd felt that odd sympathy for him when he'd been asleep on the bench, she sensed she wasn't the only one with problems. She couldn't begin to think what his problems could possibly be, though, considering who he was.

"Judd, you don't know what you'd be getting into. I'm doing you a favor by not taking you seriously. We aren't exactly run-of-the-mill housemates. Kate collects wind chimes and has them hanging all over the cottage. Her husband Roy won't let anyone else in the kitchen, and unless you like tofu, you'll starve or sneak food into your room like the rest of us do. Wayne says maybe two words all day and is what is kindly called a slob. To say the house is cluttered is understating the matter. It's not what you're used to, believe me."

His gaze never left hers as he closed the distance between them. Placing his hands on her shoulders, he said, "I'm currently staying in a plastic, pristine apartment that has overactive maid service. The most challenging conversation I've had all day has been with the doorman and a kid building a sand castle. I could visit my sister and her husband, which would mean discussing Dow Joncs averages and dodging Justine's attempts to find me the perfect woman. Since I had no choice about taking this vacation, at least I can have a choice as to who I spend it with. Let me come live with you."

Erin's practical side admitted that his temporary stay with them would solve their immediate cash-flow problem, plus give them more time to find someone else.

Her emotional side was having a bit more trouble accepting his offer. The practical side won.

Feeling as though she was committing the biggest mistake of her life, she compromised by saying, "You can come out to the house tomorrow to meet everyone and see the place. If you still want to stay after you've seen what you'd be getting into, I won't object."

He cupped her face in his hands. "I'll just come home with you tonight. I've never been very good at following directions."

"You aren't very good at taking no for an answer either."

He smiled. "Like when?"

"Like when I said I didn't want to get involved with you. I still mean it, Judd. Our group needs a housemate, not me. If you do stay with us, that doesn't mean you're welcome into my bed."

"How about kissing? Will that be allowed?"

Refusing to let him draw her into a nonsensical—

albeit intriguing—discussion about kissing, she pushed him away and went back to work. If he'd insisted on an answer, she wasn't sure what it would be. Kissing him was like taking a roller coaster ride during an electric storm.

# *Three*

After Erin drove Judd to his apartment that night, she waited for him in the living room while he packed some clothes. She didn't dare sit down for fear she might fall asleep. As she strolled around the room, she noticed how much her feet sank into the lush carpet. Glancing at her surroundings, she wondered why Judd would want to leave this plush apartment for a cluttered, extremely lived-in house crowded with four other people and their possessions. She knew her reasons for accepting him as a temporary boarder, but she couldn't understand his reasons for asking.

Her gaze roamed the spotless living room. Whoever had decorated the apartment had discarded practical furnishings for tasteful elegance. The room could have come directly out of a furniture showroom. There were no indications anyone was living there. There wasn't even an indentation in the cushions to indicate anyone had ever sat down on the white linen sofa. A single print depicting an ocean scene was the sole decoration on the cream-colored walls. A few artfully arranged plants were all that broke up the monotony of perfection.

If Judd preferred this style of living, she mused, he was in for a rude awakening when he saw the house in Haleiwa.

When he came out of one of the bedrooms carrying a suitcase, she tried to warn him again. "I don't know what you're expecting our house to be like, Judd, but this isn't it."

He stopped in front of her. "Having second thoughts, Erin?"

"I'm up to about twenty-four," she admitted. "And that was before I saw this place. If this is the type of living arrangements you like, our house is going to drive you crazy. None of us excel at neatness, except for Roy, who keeps the kitchen so immaculate you could eat off the floor. The rest of the house is sort of messy."

Amusement glittered in his eyes. "Are we talking casually sloppy or pigsty?"

"Somewhere in between. Running the gallery and taking commissions doesn't leave us much time for tidying up. Last year a friend of ours gave us a burlwood coffee table he made. I can't remember the last time I've seen the top of it."

"My shots are all up-to-date. I'll survive."

That should have relieved her conscience, but it didn't. "I thought I would do anything to keep the gallery going and to pay the rent, but I guess there are limits. I can't use you this way. I admit I need the money, but it wouldn't be fair to you when apparently you're used to living like this."

He glanced around the room. "My sister called a decorator to furnish this place right after the company purchased it. Her request was to have it designed to impress clients. It isn't meant to provide a place where you can kick your shoes off and sprawl all over the furniture." Looking at her again, he added, "I hate it."

She wasn't convinced yet. "I don't think it will work."

"Yes, it will. I'll get two weeks of sleep while I'm with you, and you'll get your rent money. We'll both get something out of this arrangement."

Her conscience still prickled like a heat rash. "If you change your mind once you see the house, there will be no hard feelings, okay? I'll refund your money." She extended her right hand. "Deal?"

Setting the suitcase down, Judd ignored her hand and placed his on her shoulders. "Deal," he murmured, then he lowered his head and covered her mouth.

Need spiraled through her with a force that snatched her breath away. She'd been attracted to a man before, but nothing compared to this devastating explosion of the senses when Judd kissed her. She was powerless to fight the sensations rushing over her as he parted her lips and deepened the assault on her mouth. As though from a distance, she heard a soft yearning sound and realized it had come from her.

He was male heat, hard strength, and searing

sensuality, all reasons why she should be resisting him. With that intent in mind, she slid her hands from his waist to his chest to push him away. Before she could put the thought into action, though, he slanted his mouth over hers to taste her more intimately.

Feeling herself sinking into a sea of desire unlike anything she'd ever experienced, Erin tore her mouth away from his.

"No, Judd. I don't want this."

Judd slowly raised his head. When he saw the dazed passion in her stunning blue eyes, he nearly pulled her back into his arms. Giving himself time to control his breathing, he lowered his gaze to her generous mouth. Moist from his kisses, her lips were a tantalizing temptation he found hard to resist. But he would. For now.

Restraint made his voice husky. Tenderness made his gaze soften. "Since I've been raised to be a gentleman, I won't call you a liar."

She reached into her back pocket for the money he'd given her for his share of the rent. Holding it out to him, she said. "Here. I've changed my mind. This won't work."

He took the folded wad of cash, but instead of keeping it, he slid it into the breast pocket of her shirt. "We made a deal, and I'm holding you to it."

Erin resisted the impulse to touch her breast where his fingers had brushed briefly against her sensitive flesh. Even through the material of her shirt, she had felt his searing touch.

"The deal included not getting involved with

each other," she said. "I'm going to hold you to that."

Judd studied her troubled expression, wondering why she was so adamant about that. "We give each other a great deal of pleasure. No matter how many different ways you want to look at it, I can't see what's wrong with that."

"I didn't say it was wrong. I just said it wasn't going to happen."

"For argument's sake, would you mind telling me why? We're attracted to each other. Hell, we burn each other up."

"Judd, it's important for me to make a success out of my career. I have to prove to myself and my four brothers that I can make it on my own. I can't let anything or anyone interfere with that."

"I don't expect to live in your back pocket, even if I can't think of any other place I'd rather be right now. I know you have work to do, and I respect that. I'm the last person to try to tell someone she shouldn't work. For the last eight years, that's all I've done. It's all I know how to do. I'm going crazy with nothing to do. I might just make it through this vacation if I can spend it with you and your friends."

"You make a vacation sound as though it's some sort of punishment. Why did you take one if you really didn't want one?"

"Doctor's order," he said grudgingly. "I've been having a little trouble sleeping, and like an idiot, I went to see my brother-in-law, who's a doctor. He recommended a vacation. I was all set to ignore his advice, but he snitched to my sister, who promptly told my other two sisters and my mother. I didn't stand a chance when they all ganged up on me."

Erin knew the feeling. There was definitely strength in numbers. Fighting her brothers' possessive natures was easier one at a time, but together they were a formidable force. It looked as though she and Judd had more in common than a strong physical attraction.

Against her better judgment, she gave in. Weariness dragged heavily on her, making it difficult for her to put up much of a fight anyway. And she still needed the money. She rationalized her decision by telling herself it would only be for two weeks. Nothing much could happen in two weeks.

"If you're ready," she said, glancing down at his suitcase, "we'd better get going. It's my turn to open the gallery in the morning, and I need to get some sleep."

As Judd bent down to pick up his suitcase, he was surprised at the feeling of relief that was washing over him. For a moment there, he'd thought she was going to refuse. It had become vitally important for him to continue seeing Erin. He didn't know why, except that he wanted her. He'd been attracted to women before, but not like this. He had to find out why.

Thirty minutes later Erin parked her minivan behind the gallery. The outdoor security lights attached to the gallery illuminated the driveway and vacant parking spaces, creating an island of artificial daylight. The small clock in the dashboard informed her it was a little after three in the morning. Even at that hour she could see light filtering through the blinds covering the living room windows. Wayne was probably wandering around as usual, since he preferred to work at night. At least Judd would have company when he had difficulty sleeping.

She turned her head to look at the man beside her. Judd had fallen asleep almost as soon as she'd driven past the city limits of Honolulu. She was going to have to wake him up, show him his room and the rest of the house, and get him settled before she could sleep herself. A couple of hours were better than none at all, although her tired body felt as though it could sleep for about a week and a half.

Sighing heavily, she lifted her hand toward Judd with the intention of waking him, but she stopped herself before she actually touched him. The yellow glow from one of the security lights illuminated his face, and she took advantage of the opportunity to study him without his knowledge. At some point during the drive he'd slipped off his glasses and put them in his shirt pocket. His long, thick lashes rested on his tanned skin; his lips were slightly parted.

What was it about this man that affected her so strangely? she wondered. Lord knows, he was an attractive man, and she'd always been susceptible to beauty in a variety of forms. But she'd met physically attractive men and didn't feel immersed in sensual heat whenever she looked at them. With just a smile in her direction, Judd could make her heart either race or feel as though it had stopped entirely. Listing all the reasons for her to fight her attraction to him wasn't necessary. There was only one. Judd was going to be on the island temporarily. Even if she were interested in becoming involved with a man, Judd Stafford couldn't be the one.

Still watching him, she thought about his proclivity for falling asleep in her company. She supposed some women would feel insulted if a man continually slept when with her. Especially if they had some kind of relationship. But she and Judd didn't have a relationship other than as landlady and tenant.

She placed her hand on his shoulder and shook him several times.

"Judd, wake up."

He mumbled something which could have been, "All right," "It's bright," "I might," or "Good night." Other than that, he didn't appear to be coming out of his sleep-induced coma.

Glaring at him didn't do much good, since his eyes were closed, but it made her feel better. "If you don't wake up, I'll leave you here," she warned. "You can spend the rest of the night in the van and wake up in the morning as twisted as a pretzel."

When her softly voiced threats didn't get any reaction either, she leaned toward him with the intention of shaking him so hard, his teeth would rattle. She never got the chance.

Strong hands clamped around her waist and lifted her over the shift console between them. She ended up sitting across his firm thighs, her skirt twisted under her, but that was the least of her problems. Pushing against his chest, she started to struggle.

"I wouldn't keep moving on me like that if I were you," he murmured, his voice low and husky with sleep and arousal, his eyes still closed.

"Then let me go."

He opened his eyes and stared at her. "If that's my only option, I'd rather you continued to wiggle on my lap. I only thought it was fair to warn you what might happen if you keep grinding against me. Let me rephrase that. That's already happening."

She could feel him growing hard and firm beneath her thigh and stopped struggling. Fighting the sensations caused by his nearness was like trying to stop a tidal wave, and she was just too tired to keep up the battle. She leaned against him and laid her head on his chest, her breath escaping from her lips in a long-drawn-out sigh.

Surprised by her sudden capitulation, Judd wrapped his arms around her and simply held her. The clean floral scent of her hair blended with the clear night air coming through the open window. She was soft and warm and infinitely precious in his arms. Three days ago he hadn't even known this woman existed. In such a short time Erin Callahan had turned him upside down and inside out, and he was beginning to wonder if it was going to be a permanent condition.

"How much sleep have you been getting lately, Erin?"

"Not enough," she said drowsily.

He could feel her warm breath through the

material of his shirt. "That's obvious. As much as I'm enjoying this, you need to get inside and get some sleep."

She nuzzled his chest as though attempting to find a more comfortable position. "In a minute. I just need a few more seconds to recharge my batteries."

"Lord knows you're charging mine," he muttered more to himself than to her.

Sensitive to the change in her breathing, he realized she was close to falling asleep. As much as he enjoyed the feel of her in his arms, he knew she would rest better in her own bed. Unfortunately, it was too soon for him to join her there. Admitting that her comfort was more important than his own selfish desire to have her in his arms was added proof his feelings for her were stronger than mere attraction.

He shifted her weight so he could reach the latch on the door, then used his foot to push the door open as far as it would go. With relative ease, he lifted Erin in his arms and got out of the van. He half expected her to protest, and his heart rocked in his chest when she buried her face in his neck and wrapped her arms around him. Her breath was warm and deliciously tormenting against his skin.

He closed his eyes as he struggled to control the surge of desire that threatened to overwhelm him. When he managed to subdue the aching need to bury himself deep inside her, he bumped the door shut with his hip and started walking toward the house.

The closed front door was a problem, considering he had both of his hands full, but the solution presented itself when he saw the shadow of a person through the curtained pane of glass in the door. Someone was walking past the door. He remembered Erin saying one of her housemates wandered around the house at night. At the time, Judd had considered the man's habit a bit unusual, considering Judd would give his Porsche for a solid night's sleep. Now he was thankful the guy was a night owl.

With his foot he nudged the door softly a couple of times to try to get the attention of the person inside. He glanced down at Erin to see if the noise disturbed her, but her eyes remained closed, her breathing slow and steady.

He tore his gaze away from her when he heard the protesting squeak of hinges as the door was pulled open. At first glance, Judd thought the person opening the door was a boy. He was at least a foot shorter than Judd's height of six feet. He was wearing a shirt that must have been two sizes too big for him, and his jeans were faded and worn. The dark stubble on his chin was the only indication that the figure in front of Judd wasn't an underdeveloped teenager.

His voice was another indication. A low rumble came from the man as he shoved open the door, his gaze on the woman in Judd's arms. "What's wrong with Erin?"

"Nothing's wrong with her. She's just asleep."

Both men heard Erin sigh deeply, as though the sigh had started from her toes. "I'm not asleep."

Raising her head, she said, "Wayne, this is Judd Stafford. He's going to stay in Polly's old room temporarily. Judd, meet Wayne Garrett."

Since Judd had his hands full, he nodded in acknowledgment of the introduction.

"Judd, you can let me down now."

"In a minute. When we get to your bedroom."

Wayne stared at Judd, his mouth dropping open slightly, then he opened the door wider so they could enter.

Judd turned sideways to ease his slender burden through the doorway and followed the short man down the hall. Wayne opened one of the bedroom doors and stepped to the side so Judd could carry Erin inside. The light from the hallway allowed him to see where he was going without bumping into any furniture. A quick glance around showed him there wasn't much to bump into anyway. In fact, her bedroom resembled what he thought would pass for a nun's closet.

Instead of a regular-size bed there was a narrow iron-framed cot that reminded him of the rusty rack he'd slept on at Camp Okiboji one summer. Other than the bed, he saw the shadowy outline of an oppressively heavy dresser. Next to the cot was a small table that resembled a plant stand with the legs cut down. A lamp with a mock Tiffany shade overpowered the top.

That was all there was in the small room. A cot, a dresser, a short plant stand, and a lamp. No rug, no chairs. No knickknacks. Nothing lying around to show that Erin lived there. There wasn't even a window. The condition of her bedroom made him wonder about the room he was going to be occupying. He hadn't taken her earlier warnings seriously. Perhaps he should have.

She made a soft sound of protest when he gently laid her on the thin mattress. He couldn't blame her. He'd do more than groan if he had to spend the night on that cot.

As soon as he released her, she started to sit up. He sat down on the edge, effectively blocking her from getting off the cot. "Where do you think you're going?"

"I need to get some clean sheets for your bed and show you around."

"Wayne can do that," he said soothingly as he brushed back a few strands of hair that had escaped from the clasp behind her head. "He's obviously wide awake. You aren't. You need to get some sleep."

"You're my responsibility, not Wayne's."

He ran a finger down her stubborn little jaw. "I can just leave and go back to Honolulu, then you wouldn't have to show me anything. Of course, then you wouldn't have the rent money, but that's your choice."

She frowned at him. "Are you going to throw that money up at me every time you want something?"

He smiled. "Just this once, I promise. I know what it's like not to get enough sleep, Erin. Use what little time you have of what's left of the night and close those beautiful eyes. If I can run a large multimillion-dollar company, I can figure out how to make a bed and find the bathroom."

Concern deepened the frown between her eyes. "What about you? Will you be able to sleep?"

"Is that an offer?" He stroked the silky skin of her throat. "I'm able to sleep when I'm with you."

She pushed his hand away. "That's about the dumbest line I've ever heard. Or wishful thinking."

"It's not a line. It's the truth. You have a very soothing effect on me, which doesn't make much sense when you also make me want to start ripping your clothes off."

Shaking her head in exasperation, Erin collapsed back on the cot. "I must have been out of my mind to agree to let you stay here."

He leaned over to remove her sandals, dropping them on the floor beside the bed. "Worry about that when you wake up."

"I think I should worry about it now, before it's too late."

He watched as her eyes closed and her breathing slowly deepened. Pushing himself off the cot, he stood over her, drinking in the sight of her like a man who'd been dying of thirst for a very long time and had finally found life-giving water.

"I have a feeling it's already too late," he murmured under his breath.

Before he gave in to the temptation to lie down beside her, he left her bedroom, quietly closing the door behind him. The narrow cot wouldn't deter him from joining her, but the fact that she wasn't ready to admit there was something between them would. When they came together, he wanted her to need him as much as he needed her. If that was possible.

Standing in the hall, he leaned back against her door, removed his glasses, and closed his eyes. They burned from lack of sleep, and he felt as though his brain was mired in quicksand.

The sound of someone clearing his throat brought his head around. A blurred figure was standing at the end of the hall. Slipping his glasses back on, he recognized the man who had let them into the house.

"Wayne. Just the person I want to see."

"You do?"

"Yes. Could you show me which is my room and where I can find clean sheets?"

"I guess so."

The room wasn't at all what Judd had expected after seeing Erin's pitifully furnished bedroom. There was a curtained window, a double bed, two dressers, a large closet, and a cool splash of color on a large canvas hanging on one wall. An oval braided rug lay on the floor next to the bed.

Wayne helped him make up the bed with clean sheets without being asked. Judd didn't try to make conversation. It had occurred to him that the other man was not antisocial but shy. The fact that Wayne preferred to have the house to himself during the night gave him the clue that the artist was more comfortable with his own company than with other people's.

Having come to that conclusion, Judd was surprised when Wayne initiated a conversation. "Do you work in oil or acrylics?" he asked.

"Neither."

"What medium do you use then?"

Stuffing a pillow into a crisp white case, Judd answered, "Components."

"Huh?"

"Electrical components."

Standing with hands on hips, Wayne stared at Judd. "You aren't an artist?"

"I can't draw a straight line."

"I don't get it. Why would Erin rent Polly's room to you if you aren't an artist?"

Judd knew it was going to be difficult enough maintaining any aspect of privacy in the cottage without having the added complication of everyone knowing his intentions were not entirely honorable.

"It's only temporary," he said vaguely. "I'll be here just a couple of weeks."

Wayne's expression didn't change. He was still obviously puzzled about the arrangements Erin had made. Instead of asking more questions, though, he muttered an invitation to share a cold drink as he walked toward the door.

Judd agreed and followed Wayne out into the hall.

"That's the bathroom," Wayne said, pointing to the first door on the left. "Next to it is Roy and Kate's room. Mine's across the hall. I advise you to take your turn in the bathroom before seven in the morning. That's when Kate's alarm goes off. Erin's usually up and about earlier, and she doesn't hog the bathroom the way Kate does. Once Kate takes possession, no one stands a chance of crossing the threshold for a long time."

"I'll remember that," Judd murmured. Having

lived with two or more women for a number of years, he was familiar with the phenomenon of the female bathroom ritual.

Wayne gestured for him to go into the living room, and Judd sat down on the plump cushion on one of the dark green rattan chairs.

While waiting for Wayne to return from wherever he'd gone, he looked around. He hadn't paid any attention to his surroundings when he'd carried Erin through the house to her bedroom, and was pleasantly impressed by the homey atmosphere created by the rattan couch, chairs, and end tables. Paintings in a variety of styles adorned the walls, evidently samples of all the occupants' work. Healthy plants and attractive pottery blended with the green, peach, and light blue fabric on the cushions.

The mess that Erin had warned him about was evident by the clutter in the room, but it wasn't anything he couldn't live with. There were various art magazines, pieces of clothing, books, several woodcarvings in progress, and candles scattered about.

He leaned his head against the back of the chair and stretched his long legs out in front of him, enjoying the peaceful room and the cooling breeze coming through the open louvered windows. The wind chimes Erin had mentioned were hanging from the ceiling in several places and were gently disturbed by the current of fresh air. The soft melodious clatter was soothing rather than irritating.

He was satisfied with the evening's events, Judd

mused. He had found a way into Erin's private life and would be able to see her more often.

He would also be able to get some sleep.

Wayne entered the room carrying two glasses. He handed one to Judd, then hovered near the couch as though unsure what he was supposed to do next.

"Thanks." Judd took a tentative sip of the peach-colored drink. "What is this?"

"Guava juice."

Judd couldn't think of a single thing to say about the unusually flavored drink, so he said, "Erin told me you work at night."

Wayne's slight nod wasn't encouraging, but Judd gave it another try. "If you wouldn't mind taking a few more minutes from your work, I'd like to ask you a couple of questions."

Judd could see curiosity battle with caution in the other man's expression and waited.

Finally, Wayne sat down at the farthest end of the couch and balanced his glass on his knee. "What do you want to know?"

"Why is Erin living like Cinderella in this house?"

The other man blinked, then after a moment smiled. "You mean her room?" Judd nodded. "She handles the financial end of things," Wayne explained. "She doesn't begrudge spending money on furnishings for everyone but herself."

"Why?"

Wayne shrugged. "Why don't you ask her?"

"She's sleeping."

Wayne frowned in bewilderment. "What's the

rush? You could ask her whatever you want to know in the morning."

"Would she tell me?"

The timid smile returned. "Maybe not. She's got this thing about being independent. She doesn't volunteer much about herself."

Judd had noticed. He wanted to take advantage of Wayne's willingness to answer his questions about Erin, but before he could ask another question, the artist gulped down his drink and stood.

"I'll be at the studio attached to the gallery if you need anything. You can find me by going out the back door and turning left."

Judd glanced at his watch. It was almost four o'clock in the morning. And he didn't feel at all as though he could sleep. Letting Wayne off the hook, he said, "Thanks for your help."

Wayne nodded brusquely. "No problem. I guess I'll be seeing you around." He took a couple of steps away from the couch then turned and asked, "Do any of Erin's brothers know about your staying here?"

"I doubt it. Does it matter?"

"It might." Surprisingly, he grinned. "They're going to love this."

Judd's gaze followed the artist as he left the room, a frown creasing his forehead. What the hell was that all about? he wondered.

Leaning his head back again, he let the silence flow over him and shut his burning eyes. He smiled as he thought about how his sister Justine would react when he called her to tell her where he was staying. Somehow he was going to have to convince her he hadn't lost what was left of his mind. It wasn't going to be easy, considering he wasn't the type of person to make any sort of decision without first weighing every option. Justine was going to think it odd that he'd left the condo on the spur of the moment to take up residence in an artist's colony. The closest he'd ever been to artwork had been when he'd pounded a nail in a wall to hang a painting.

He pushed himself out of the chair and walked down the hall to his room. He passed Erin's door without giving in to the temptation to look in on her. After softly closing his door, he kicked off his shoes and lay down on top of the quilt spread over the bed. Placing his hands behind his head, he stared up at the ceiling, thinking about the woman sleeping across the hall.

Just knowing she was only a short distance away gave him a feeling of satisfaction and peace, as though a missing piece of a puzzle had been fitted into place.

He shifted a number of times, trying to find a comfortable position. He punched the pillow and arranged it several different ways. Nothing helped. It was like so many other nights when he hadn't been able to sleep, and he wasn't taking this one any better than he had the others.

After a few more frustrating minutes of staring at the dark ceiling, he made a low growling sound and swung his long legs over the side of the bed.

His bare feet made no sound on the wooden floor as he crossed the room to the door. He opened it quietly and stepped across the hall.

# Four

Erin fastened her long hair in a ponytail as she walked quickly down the hallway toward the kitchen. She'd overslept. Again. This was becoming a habit, one she couldn't afford.

This time it hadn't been because she'd forgotten to set her alarm or had shut it off and gone back to sleep. She hadn't even been able to find the darn clock when she'd finally opened her eyes. It wasn't where it was supposed to be on her nightstand.

That wasn't the only unusual thing she'd noticed. Her cot had been moved away from the wall. She didn't remember doing that, but she must have. Who else would have done it?

Nearly falling off the cot in the process of rolling over was what had eventually awakened her. She vaguely remembered turning toward that side of the cot to search for the warmth she'd expected to be there. Once she was fully awake, she couldn't understand why she had sought warmth next to her when there was a perfectly good blanket at the foot of the cot.

Unless it was because she'd been dreaming she'd been lying in Judd's arms.

The door to the room Judd had been given was open, the bed made. She'd seen his suitcase sitting on the floor at the foot of the bed as she'd passed by the room, proof she hadn't been dreaming about renting Polly's room to Judd Stafford.

Tucking her white cotton tank top into the waistband of her madras print skirt, she entered the kitchen, expecting to see her housemates gathered around the table. She stopped just inside the doorway and looked around. The room was immaculately clean, the counters clear, the large picnic-style table bare of the usual morning clutter of plates, cups, and coffee. Touching the side of the empty coffeepot, she felt coolness, not residual heat.

She glanced at the wall clock to confirm her suspicions that it must be later than she thought. She looked again. That can't be right, she thought, shaking her head as though to clear it. The small hand was on ten and the large hand was on six. She was supposed to open the gallery at nine, and the clock was telling her she was an hour and a half late.

Apparently, Kate had opened the gallery, although Kate had been planning to go to a client's house that morning to assist in the hanging of one of her paintings. They all had their particular jobs to do, and it wasn't unusual for them to prod one another when something wasn't being done. For some reason, though, no one had wakened her that morning.

Rather than wait for coffee to brew, she opened the refrigerator and took out a small can of apple juice. She pulled off the foil tab as she left the house.

Her sandals lightly crunched on the gravel under her feet as she crossed the parking area, heading for the back door of the gallery. Several cars were parked near the front entrance, which meant there were customers. Mornings were usually a little slow during the week, unless it was a rainy day. Tourists tended to spend more time looking into indoor activities when the sun wasn't shining.

Erin heard the loud concussion of a staple gun as she entered the workshop in the back of the gallery. Roy was bending over a frame he was putting together, his muscular arms holding the heavy frame easily. With his tanned, beach-boy good looks and tall, athletic body, he looked like he'd be more at home on a surfboard or wielding a hammer than executing delicate watercolor paintings of island children.

When he finished attaching one side of the frame, he looked up and grinned at Erin. "Hi. So you finally decided to join the living."

She didn't return his smile. "Why didn't someone wake me up?"

"Judd said to let you sleep."

"Judd?"

Roy nodded. "He said you were exhausted and

needed to catch up on some sleep. We've noticed how tired you've been lately and decided he was right, so we didn't wake you."

Erin's fingers gripped the edge of the worktable, as if she were trying to hold on to her temper physically. "Judd Stafford is a temporary boarder. He has no say in what I do."

"Even when he's right? You've been pushing yourself too hard for too long, Erin. Judd's made us realize we've been taking advantage of you. We all want to make Hale Hana a success, but none of us work as hard at it as you do."

"I'm not working any harder than the rest of you." Switching the subject, she said, "I need to go relieve Kate in the gallery. We'll talk about this later. All of us, including Mr. Stafford."

"Kate's not in the gallery. She had an appointment to hang a painting in a client's home."

Erin frowned. With Polly gone, that left Wayne to fill in at the gallery, and Wayne resisted having to deal with the public. He would rather walk barefoot over ground glass than wait on customers.

Leaving the workroom, Erin swept open the swinging door that separated the two different parts of the gallery and walked into the showroom. Several tourists were wandering around looking at the paintings displayed on the walls and the partitions Wayne and Roy had constructed to give them more hanging space.

Rounding one of the partitions in order to reach the main counter, she stopped abruptly when she saw the man who was sitting on the high stool behind the counter. He was leaning against the wall behind him, his arms crossed casually over his chest. His green eyes glittered with amusement when he spotted her, but he didn't move.

Erin slowly walked toward Judd, aware of the way his gaze followed her every step, noted each breath she took. It was that blatant awareness that had unsettled her from the first moment they'd met. Whether it was his intention or not, he made her feel very female, very special. Right now, that was even harder to combat than the ever-present physical attraction arcing between them.

She walked around to the front of the counter, intentionally keeping it between them, and reached for a piece of candy in the small basket sitting on the counter. In order to unwrap it, she had to set her can of juice down.

Judd glanced at the juice. "Apple juice and butterscotch candy?" he asked. "That's not exactly the approved breakfast of champions."

"Thanks to you, I missed breakfast."

"You're welcome," he said unabashedly. "I, on the other hand, valiantly made my way through a stack of Roy's rice flour pancakes, fried bananas, and herbal tea."

"That must be why Roy went along with your suggestion to let me sleep. How did you get around the others?"

"It must be my natural charm." He studied her carefully. "Are you really as mad as you sound, or just cranky because you didn't get any coffee?"

She met his gaze squarely. "Don't you think I have a right to be mad? It was my turn to open the gallery this morning, and it's because of your telling my partners not to wake me that I didn't. You might be on vacation, but I'm not. I take my responsibilities seriously, even if you don't."

One of the customers was gesturing for Judd's attention. The front legs of the stool hit the floor as he leaned forward, placing his hands on the counter. "I take my responsibilities seriously too, Erin," he said softly. "I take care of the woman I sleep with. That's why I took your alarm clock when I left your bed this morning so you would sleep without any interruptions."

Her mouth dropped open, and she made a strangled sound. "You don't sleep with me."

"I did last night. It was the best couple of hours' sleep I've had in a long time." His gaze shifted to the customer, who was looking at him expectantly. "Excuse me, sweetheart. I'm going to sell that woman a painting."

Still shocked, Erin watched as he calmly sauntered over to the woman who was standing in front of one of her paintings. She raised her hand as though to make a point, then left it fall back to her side. Throwing both hands up in the air, she stormed out of the gallery into the back room.

She stood in the workroom for a moment, turned around to go back into the gallery, took one step, then stopped and turned again. She took two steps toward the back door, only to whirl around to face the door to the gallery.

"Is this some kind of new mating dance?"

She jerked her head around. Roy was standing in front of the workbench with his hands on his hips, grinning broadly.

"This isn't funny," she said. "We have a crazy man living in the house, and it's all my fault."

"You mean Judd? He's not crazy. He fits in just fine."

"You're only saying that because he ate your rice pancakes."

Roy laughed. "That does prove that he's a man of discriminating taste, but that isn't what I meant. He's going to help us build the addition to the showroom and has some good ideas as to how we can save money on materials. When he first told me he wasn't an artist, I thought he might be dead wood around here. But after a few minutes of talking with him, he impressed me as a man who could contribute something to the group."

Erin had to agree with Roy. Judd was contributing a great deal to her inventory of problems. At the moment, he was right at the top of the list.

Her main problem spoke from behind her. "Erin, this lady wants to buy one of your paintings. Do we take credit cards?"

She slowly turned to face Judd. Mentally throwing up her hands in defeat, she walked toward him. Running away from her problems had never been her way. She wasn't going to start now.

"Yes, we do," she said sweetly, emphasizing the same pronoun he'd stressed.

He looked at her a little warily, as if puzzled by her change in attitude. "Someone's going to have to show me how to work that little machine, then."

"You mean there's something you don't know how to do?" she asked, stopping beside him.

He didn't move aside so she could pass through

the doorway, and she looked up at him questioningly.

His smile was warm and intimate. "I'm always open to new experiences."

She stepped closer. He still didn't move. She squeezed into the small space between him and the door frame.

Placing her hands on his solid chest, she gave it a couple of consoling pats. "Then you'll love learning how to work the charge machine. It'll open up a whole new world for you."

"You've already done that."

The low timbre of his voice sent shivers down her spine. Before she got into even more trouble, she slid through the narrow space, sucking in her breath as she felt his hard frame rub against hers. She raised her gaze to meet his and saw the heated desire flaring in the depths of his eyes.

The loud retort of the staple gun broke the spell weaving around them, and Erin brushed by Judd. It was becoming harder and harder to escape the tumultuous feelings he aroused deep within her, she thought as she walked toward the woman waiting near the counter.

After the painting was paid for, wrapped up, and sent out the door with its new owner, Erin entered the sale in the ledger. While she was bent over the counter, she tried to figure out the best way to put what she had to say to Judd. He usually managed to twist anything she said to mean something else. She needed to make herself crystal clear without any chance of being misunderstood. Judd was making assumptions he had no right to make about her. Even if he was only teasing, she had to make him stop insinuating there was anything between them.

She shut the ledger and turned around to face him, even though she hadn't come up with any great strategy. It would have helped if he'd been looking at her instead of staring at the door. Then he walked past her and around the counter, never once glancing at her on his way toward the entrance.

Her mouth dropped open in astonishment as he walked out of the gallery. She recognized the woman who was two steps away from the door when Judd whirled her around and forced her back the other way. The woman was Justine Garrison, Judd's sister.

Through the screen door Erin could see Judd gesture toward the gallery with one hand as he held his sister's arm with the other, keeping her in front of him as he obviously argued with her.

When the phone on the counter rang, Erin pulled her attention away from the strange tableau outside and answered it. She nearly groaned out loud when she recognized her brother's voice.

"Hello, Patrick," she said. "What's up?"

Justine squinted against the sun as she looked up at her brother. "Judd, could we go inside to have this little discussion? I'm going to get sunstroke out here."

Judd glanced down at his sister's daffodil-yellow suit and print blouse, which was more appropriate for the air-conditioned Stafford Building than standing in the sun-baked parking lot.

"Your limo is even closer," he said. "Why don't you just hop into it and drive back to Honolulu? You can report to Mom and the other girls that I'm just fine. I know exactly what I'm doing."

Justine shielded her eyes from the sun with her hand. "And what exactly are you doing?"

Judd glanced back toward the gallery. He could see Erin's shadowy outline through the mesh of the front screen door. "I'm relaxing," he said, bringing his gaze back to his sister. "Isn't that what I'm supposed to be doing?"

"In the condo. With us. Or on the beach. Not here in the middle of the island at some artist's colony. When you called and told me you were here, I almost phoned Mother and the girls to tell them I was sending the men in the white coats after you because you had flipped your lid."

"I'm glad you restrained yourself," he said dryly. "That's just what I need, all the Stafford women hovering over Erin. She's skittish enough as it is."

Justine dropped her hand and stared at her brother. "Erin? You mean Erin Callahan, the girl who's painting the mural in the lobby? Is that what all this is about? You want to have a little fling with some island girl? If it's companionship you want, there's this wonderful woman I think you should meet. Her name is Resina Bucham. She's a brilliant chemist, very pretty and charming."

Judd looked skyward as though beseeching the heavens in his time of need. He also wondered how many years he would get for throttling one of his own flesh and blood.

Striving for patience, he took a deep, steadying breath. "I'm not interested in meeting any of your girl wonders, Justine. And I'm not having a little fling with Erin. Meeting Erin has made this vacation endurable. I only called you so you wouldn't worry and call out the National Guard to look for me. As you can see, I'm perfectly all right."

His sister glanced at the gallery, then back at him. "But, Judd, here? I doubt if they even have air-conditioning. Come back to the condo. You'll be able to rest properly. You can't be comfortable here."

"You'd be surprised," he drawled.

Justine started to ask another question, but he had had enough. Taking her arm, he drew her over to her gray limousine. Waving the chauffeur away, he opened the door for his sister and helped her inside.

Bending down, he tried to reassure her once again. "I'll give you a call in a couple of days. Try to stay off the trans-Pacific phones lines, okay? The last thing I need is to have the rest of the family treating me like a six-year-old."

"That's not what I'm doing, Judd. We love you and worry about you."

Leaning forward, he kissed his sister's cheek. "I know," he said gently. "I love you all too. That's why I put up with you interfering in my life."

He started to straighten up, but Justine grasped his hand. "Erin Callahan must be fairly special for you to go through this much trouble in order to be with her."

He squeezed her hand and smiled. "It's no trouble at all."

Erin replaced the phone receiver with exaggerated care, as though it were made of hand-blown crystal. It would have been much more satisfying to slam it down, but that wouldn't accomplish anything—other than giving her an outlet for her frustration at trying to convince any of her brothers that she was capable of managing on her own.

She looked up when she heard the bell hanging on the door clang against the wood. She saw Judd looking at her hand and realized he'd seen the way she'd hung up the phone.

"It's probably wrong of me to criticize you," she said, "considering we aren't paying you, but you don't seem to understand the concept of working in a gallery. You're supposed to encourage people to come in and browse around, not shove them out the door."

"My sister just wanted to tell me she thought I was crazy."

"I've told you that and you didn't shove me out the door."

He walked toward her. "I was actually doing you a favor. If my sister came in here and saw you, she would start tuning up her *Hello, Dolly* routine. She and my other sisters have matchmaking down to a fine science. She'd have us wedded, bedded, and expecting our first child if it was up to her."

Erin choked. Clearing her throat, she said huskily, "I hope you set her straight."

"Hopefully enough to keep my other sisters from hopping on a plane to have me committed. The women in my family tend to think they know what I need in my life more than I do."

"Your sisters should meet my brothers. They have something in common." Glancing at the phone, she muttered, "I just finished talking to my brother Patrick. He wanted me to come over to his house for a special dinner tonight, which means he has another prospect lined up for me, who will just happen to be sitting across the dinner table from me."

Judd reached over to run his finger along the side of her face. "I hope you told him you couldn't make it."

She moved so he was no longer touching her. It disconcerted her to realize it was more difficult to step away from him than it would have been to step toward him.

Picking up the ledger, she held it against her chest like a shield. "I told him I had to work, but as usual he didn't consider that an adequate reason. His exact words were that dinner with his family was more important than indulging in my hobby, as my brothers refer to my painting."

"Haven't your brothers ever seen your work?" Judd asked in surprise.

"Of course. They think my paintings are very pretty."

He flinched. "Ouch. Talk about being damned with faint praise."

She shrugged. "It's kind of funny if you think about it. Both of our families want us to stop working except yours only wants you to take some time off temporarily. Mine wants me to quit working altogether, get married, have two children, and live happily ever after safely shut up in a cottage with a white picket fence."

"I can take a vacation for a couple of weeks without it affecting my work to any extent. My work isn't who I am, but your painting is part of you. It's not the same thing at all."

Erin looked away for a moment. A man she'd known such a short time understood her better than her own brothers.

"Michael keeps hoping my painting is just a temporary phase I'm going through, like puberty was, and that I'll eventually come to my senses."

"Michael is one of your brothers?"

"He's my oldest brother. He became our mother, father, and general dictator when our parents were killed in a car accident. He was only eighteen at the time and in his first year in the navy. It couldn't have been an easy task for him to be suddenly responsible for three younger brothers and a ten-year-old girl who'd been injured in the accident."

Judd frowned in concern. "You were with your parents when they were killed?"

She nodded. "The boys had gone to a movie with some friends and my parents had picked me up from a birthday party. A drunk driver slammed into our car."

"Were you seriously hurt?"

"As you can see, I'm fine," she replied, deliberately not answering his question directly.

He tilted his head to one side. "You know, I can understand how Michael feels. Having the responsibility for my sisters and my mother wasn't always easy. My sisters, especially, didn't always agree with some of my decisions, but occasionally unpopular decisions have to be made."

"Did your sisters always do everything you told them to do?"

He chuckled. "Lord, no. They fought me capped tooth and manicured nail."

Erin smiled faintly. "And you miss the battles."

"Do I? I thought I was darn glad to be free of them at last."

"I think you're having the same problem Michael is having."

"Which problem is that?"

"Letting go. Even when I went to college, Michael insisted I live with Patrick and his wife, Stella, here on the island. He still checks up on me and is waiting for me to fall on my face so he can pick me up and dust me off and tell me 'I told you so.'"

"Or maybe it's his way of showing you he cares."

"Maybe," she conceded. "What about you?"

"What about me?"

"You don't miss the responsibility of your sisters?"

"No way. I was the happiest man alive when the last woman in my family got married. I'm free as the wind."

"And full of hot air. You're so happy you now have insomnia."

"That's because I was working too hard and needed a break."

The bell over the door clanged as two customers came in. Erin smiled at them, then glanced back at Judd.

"Enough about family problems. My brothers' protests about my working will be moot if I don't pay attention to gallery business."

Retreat came in many forms, and Judd recognized Erin's version for what it was. He was willing to let her get away with it for now, because she'd given him something to think about. "Okay. So what do you want me to do?"

She shook her head. "You're on vacation, remember? You can take my car to the beach if you'd like. I won't need it until I go to the Stafford Building at six-thirty." She picked up a pad of notepaper and a pencil from the counter. "I'll give you directions to some of the closer beaches."

He took the pencil out of her hand. "I'm not going to need directions. I'm staying right here."

That wasn't what she wanted to hear. "You'll just be bored, Judd. There are a lot of fantastic things to see on the island that would be a lot more fun than hanging around here."

He could have argued that point, but he didn't. "I promised to help Roy once you showed up to take over in the gallery." He leaned over and kissed her, effectively stopping the protest she was about to make. "I'll see you at lunch. Roy said he's fixing something with tofu, bamboo shoots, mushrooms, and a couple of other things I can't remember. Or blocked out on purpose."

Erin watched him as he strolled toward the door leading to the backroom. Maybe she had a fever, she thought, touching her forehead with one hand. That would explain why she felt as though she were floating several inches off the ground. She'd better get her feet firmly back on the ground, or the next two weeks were going to be a year long.

# Five

Erin was surprised at how easily Judd fit into the chaotic household. While she painted or worked in the gallery, he helped Wayne and Roy construct the addition onto the main building. When Judd wasn't helping someone else, he took on a number of chores on his own—mowing the lawn, rearranging the storeroom of art supplies, and washing every window in the cottage and gallery.

He remained busy constantly, approaching each activity with a concentrated intensity that made Erin marvel at his energy. After seeing him move from one project to another without pause, she could understand how finding himself with nothing to do on his forced vacation had driven him crazy.

He even showed an interest in learning how to make frames, working alongside Roy when he could find the time. He became Kate's friend for life when he fashioned an electrical device to make one of her crystal mobiles turn slowly, catching the sunlight from the windows. The one activity he wisely avoided was helping Roy in the kitchen.

Half the time, Erin felt as though she were operating in slow motion while Judd was in fast forward. Due to the minimal amount of sleep she was getting, her energy level sagged badly, like a much-used hammock. She resorted to drinking coffee in the afternoon to give her a badly needed boost.

One afternoon she ventured into the kitchen to brew a pot of coffee, hoping a cup or two would get her through the rest of the day and the long night ahead. As she was pouring her first cup, Judd spoke her name behind her, startling her. Her hand jerked, and some of the hot coffee spilled onto her other hand. She'd no sooner made a sound of surprise and pain than Judd was right beside her, lifting her hand and examining it.

"As jumpy as you are," he said, an edge of irritation in his voice, "I don't think you should drink any more of that coffee."

"You startled me," she said defensively. "I thought you were helping Roy and Wayne."

He maneuvered her over to the sink and turned on the cold water faucet. "I was. Then I saw you leave the gallery and head for the cottage."

She looked down at her hand as he held it under the stream of cold water. "This isn't necessary. I wasn't burned."

Positioning himself behind her, he wouldn't allow her to draw her hand away. "Your skin is red where the coffee spilled on your hand. Leave it under the water for a few minutes."

Erin really didn't have much choice. She was pinned against the counter with his long body pressing against her from shoulder to thigh. The discomfort from the scalding coffee was nothing compared to the heat searing her blood. Her breathing quickened at the feel of his fingers stroking her hand.

She closed her eyes and relaxed against him, her head falling back on his shoulder.

She heard his soft intake of breath. Her hand was released as he grasped her at her waist. It was her turn to gasp when she felt his damp hands on her bare skin as he slid them under her crop top. How odd, she mused hazily, that his cool, wet hands seemed to burn her.

"Judd," she said huskily, "I don't think this is helping my hand at all."

He bent his head to touch her neck with his lips. "Maybe not, but it's doing wonders for me. I can't resist the feel of you in my arms."

"I need to get back to work, Judd."

"You work too hard," he murmured against her throat.

"This from the man who was forced to take a vacation and is having trouble sleeping."

Lifting his head, he loosened his hold and turned her around to face him. He kept her close to his body, clasping his hands behind her. "Why do you work so hard, Erin? When my father died, I had to work long hours in order to get the company out of the mess he'd left it in. I had the added incentive of needing to provide for my mother and sisters. But you spend almost every waking minute doing the work of four people. Why?"

"I don't do the work of four people. Everyone else works just as hard as I do."

"You do the account books, the buying, the scheduling, make sure everyone else is comfortable at your own expense, work until the wee hours of the morning, and squeeze in your painting in what little spare time you have. None of your other partners drive themselves as hard as you do."

She leaned back as far as his arms would let her, her movement inadvertently bringing her lower body snugly against his. There was an odd breathlessness in her voice as she answered his question with a question.

"In dealing with your sisters, did you ever find that when you wanted them to do one thing one particular way, they purposely went one hundred and eighty degrees in the other direction?"

He smiled. "Most of the time."

"Aside from the fact that painting is what I've always wanted to do with my life, a career in art isn't what my oldest brother considered a reasonable choice. I've been told over and over again that I couldn't make a living with my artwork. I think I can."

"I don't have a problem with that. My only objection is that you're wearing yourself out trying to do so much. Is there some sort of deadline you feel you have to meet?"

"Only my own." She lowered her gaze to the area

of his shirt where her hand had left a dark wet spot. "Which means I need to get back to work now."

"I'll let you go if you promise to take it a little easier. There's a short distance between pushing yourself a little and too far."

Smoothing her fingers over the damp spot as though to erase it, she said, "I promise to do whatever I have to do."

Judd sighed heavily and dropped his hands, though the expression in his eyes indicated it was the last thing he wanted to do.

"That isn't quite what I was hoping for," he said, "but I guess it's all I'm going to get for now."


Judd insisted on accompanying Erin each night when she went to the Stafford Building to work on the mural. She tried talking him out of going with her, but he was always waiting for her by her van when she came out of the cottage. He was unobtrusive and undemanding as she painted. Occasionally he dozed while sitting on the bench with his back against the wall. But mostly they talked.

The evening after their tête-à-tête in the kitchen, she learned more about how he had been forced to take over the reins of Stafford Industries at the age of twenty-four, struggling to keep the company afloat after his father had drained most of its resources. Perhaps if he'd been any other type of man, Erin mused, he would never have been able to accomplish all he'd done over the years.

It was after he'd related several incidents involving his sisters' dating that she knew he missed those times with his family. Even though he told the stories with wry humor, she got the impression he'd enjoyed being needed by his family.

She asked a few subtle questions and learned his insomnia had started shortly after his youngest sister's wedding. She was the last sister to be married, to no longer be under his protective wing. Instead of wallowing in the freedom, Judd had started to battle with insomnia. It was a curious reaction. Erin kept her opinions to herself, though.

She found Judd's presence to be both comfortable and stimulating, and she was actually getting used to that odd contradiction. As long as she remembered that their friendship was only temporary, she thought she would be able to keep a proper perspective with him. They each were benefiting from the arrangement they'd made. To Erin's surprise, the arrangement was working out better than she expected.

Except when Judd came to her room in the small hours of the morning, unable to sleep.

It had started the second night he'd been at the cottage. She had fallen asleep as soon as her head hit the pillow. As tired as she was, nothing short of an earthquake should have roused her. Still, something dragged her out of the depths of sleep. Opening her eyes, she saw a shadowy figure sitting at the foot of her cot.

Even though she couldn't see his features clearly, she immediately knew who it was. Judd had removed his shirt but was still wearing his jeans. As she watched him, he ran his fingers through his hair, and she heard him sigh heavily.

"What's wrong, Judd?" she murmured. "Can't you sleep?"

"Not in there," he said softly. "Not without you."

Something clenched painfully in her chest when she heard the quiet desperation in his voice. She sensed he hated being helpless against his inability to sleep. He was a man accustomed to maintaining control over his business, his entire life, and being unable to sleep angered him.

Several seconds ticked by as she studied his profile. Then she swung her legs over the side of the cot and stood up. The tail of her cotton nightshirt fell against her bare thighs as she took the few steps that brought her to Judd.

He tilted his head back to look up at her, his face still in shadow. Then he looked down at her hand as she extended it toward him.

He placed his own hand in hers and watched as her fingers tightened their hold. When she pulled gently, he stood up. She stepped back, and he took a step forward. His gaze never left her face as she stepped backward again, leading him out of her room, across the hall, and into the bedroom he'd left earlier to seek her out.

Stopping near the bed, she said quietly. "Lie down."

He shook his head. "I tried that. It didn't work. Why do you think I ended up in your room? I was about to slip into bed with you like I did last night, but you woke up."

She placed her hands on his shoulders and

pressed him down onto the mattress. "This bed is bigger."

"You're going to sleep with me here?"

"I'll stay with you until you fall asleep."

He shook his head again. "This isn't fair to you. You're losing sleep because of me."

"Sometimes life isn't fair," she said ruefully.

He responded to the pressure of her hands and lay back onto the mattress. When he realized she wasn't joining him on the bed, he turned his head on the pillow to look at her. She was sitting next to his hip, rubbing her hand over his chest in a soothing motion.

At least, Judd thought, she probably meant the gesture to be soothing. However, her touch was doing invigorating things to his system.

The room was dark and intimate, the only illumination from the security lights beyond the window.

He covered her hand with his. "I've been trying to figure out what it is about you that conquers my insomnia."

Erin could feel his steady heartbeat under her hand. "And what conclusion did you come up with?"

"I'm still working on it. I think part of it is I must trust you if I can fall asleep when I'm with you. When someone is asleep, they're very vulnerable. Evidently I feel safe with you. There aren't all that many women I can say that about. Most of the other women I know, including the ones in my family, would help themselves to my wallet the minute I shut my eyes."

She withdrew her hand from under his. "I think you'd better think some more. You've forgotten that I took money from you for rent for this room."

When she started to rise, he clasped his fingers around her wrist. "It's not the same thing. You've been up-front with me from the beginning. No subterfuge, no games, no tears or recriminations. Just honesty. It's a refreshing change."

It wasn't his hold on her wrist that kept her beside him. It was the drowsy note in his voice. "So you think having trouble with women is the reason you're having trouble sleeping?"

He yawned. "I don't think that's it. I've had trouble with the women in my family for as long as I can remember, and it never affected my ability to sleep before."

His hold on her arm relaxed. Gently twisting free of his grip, she took his hand in hers.

Lowering her voice, she asked, "I can't imagine someone as nice as Mrs. Garrison giving you any trouble."

Judd's eyes closed, opened briefly, then closed again. "She is nice, and thankfully, she's now Travis Garrison's problem."

"And your other sisters?"

"Their husbands' problems. Even my mother's remarried. I'm finally free."

He didn't sound too happy about that, Erin mused. She didn't say that, though.

"Not all women are looking for men to support them," she said instead. "There are women who want to make their own way without any help from anyone, especially a man. In fact, some women even insist on it."

He made a scoffing sound. "I bet you also believe in Santa Claus."

"I do," she whispered. She believed in happy endings, too, but there wouldn't be one with Judd. There would be an ending, and it would not be happy. At least not for her.

She saw his chest rise and fall as he took a deep, soulful breath, then his head relaxed against the pillow. She smiled. She'd accomplished what she'd set out to do. He'd fallen asleep.

When she tried to draw her hand away, he tightened his fingers around hers, refusing to let go of her even in sleep. Using her other hand, she tried to pry his hold loose, but still he wouldn't release her. She would have to wait a little while until he fell into a deeper sleep and relaxed his grip.

While she waited, she thought about what he'd said. From what he'd told her, she gathered he expected all women to be after him for his money. She had taken money from him as well, but he didn't seem to put her in the same category as the other women in his life.

She looked away. Maybe it would be better if he did. Like her brothers, he probably wouldn't understand why she had to make a success out of a small gallery and her own career. A bid for independence made sense to her, but unfortunately not to anyone else.

Straightening her spine, she shifted a little, trying to find a more comfortable position. She shook her head in bemusement. Wouldn't her brothers have a major fit if they could see her now? She was sitting on a bed beside a man she'd known only a couple of days. It would be a toss-up whether she would be sent to a nunnery before or after her brothers tore Judd into little pieces.

They wouldn't believe her reason for being there, that she was sitting on a bed holding the hand of an attractive man in the middle of the night, because she could put him to sleep. She was finding it a little difficult to believe herself.

And she was losing sleep along with her mind. She yawned and ran her fingers through her hair. She'd give him a couple of minutes more, then she'd go back to her own room.

The next thing Erin knew she was waking up next to Judd.

When she opened her eyes, she saw the room was lighter, with sunshine shining through the drapes. Judd was firm and solid against her back as she lay on her side, his arm around her waist. She closed her eyes as she felt his warm breath on her neck. Shivers of awareness rippled and twisted along every nerve ending.

Oh, help, she thought as she fought her body's response. Her heart's response.

As carefully as she could, she eased out from under his arm and out of his bed, swearing to herself not to be such a sucker for a sad pair of sleepy eyes again.

It was easy to make such a vow, but hard to carry it out when Judd ended up in her bedroom again in the wee hours of the following morning. Unable to resist his need for her, she took his hand and led him back across the hall for a repeat of the preceding night.

The problem was, helping Judd get some sleep meant she wasn't getting much rest herself. Keeping her part of the bargain was costing her more than she could afford as the week progressed.

By the time they returned to the cottage at three o'clock early Sunday morning, Erin was too tired to be cautious, sensible, or any of the other logical things she should be. All she could think about was sleep, glorious, close-your-eyes-and-fade-into-oblivion sleep.

She walked down the hall behind Judd, then followed him into his bedroom instead of going into her own.

He didn't notice until he was already unbuttoning his shirt. He stopped and stared at her.

Kicking off her sandals, Erin sank down on the side of the bed. She lifted a pillow, punched it several times, then fluffed it before setting it back near the headboard. Satisfied, she shifted on the mattress and lay down.

Judd couldn't stop staring at her. "What are you doing?"

Turning her head on the pillow, she met his astonished gaze. "Instead of going to my room, getting three minutes of sleep, waking up to find you sitting on my bed, I decided to eliminate a few steps and come directly in here."

After watching her for a few seconds more, he shrugged off his shirt. "It makes sense to me."

She frowned, bewildered by his casual tone. He

was acting as though it were perfectly natural for them to go to bed together. Well, if he could be so casual about it, so could she.

His gaze roamed over her jeans and butter-colored chamois shirt. "Are you going to sleep in your clothes?"

She could have easily fallen asleep wearing a suit of armor, she thought. "Changing into a night-gown would require me to move," she murmured. She rolled onto her side so her back was to him. "Good night."

Judd was grinning as he shucked off his jeans and tossed them aside. He couldn't care less what her reasons were for curling up in his bed, as long as she was where he wanted her to be.

The mattress gave under his weight as he lay down on his side of the bed. He touched her gently, urging her around to face him.

Her sleepy eyes opened. "What are you doing?"

"Shh," he said soothingly as he brushed a kiss over her forehead. "It's all right. I'm just saying good night."

When she parted her lips to question his intent, he covered her mouth with his own. He took his time tasting her. It seemed like years since he'd kissed her, and his restraint had nearly driven him crazy the past few days. He didn't want to miss a single moment of this kiss. She made a soft yearning sound, and he slanted his mouth over hers, deepening the tender assault. His arm tight-ened around her waist, his hand smoothing over her back to bring her against his hard frame.

"You feel so good," he murmured against her

throat as he slid his lips over her silky skin. "You taste so good."

"Judd," she sighed, her body trembling.

Raising up on his elbow, he looked down at her. He trailed his fingers over the side of her face, to her neck, then slid his hand lower. He smiled when she opened her eyes and he saw the glow of arousal in them.

His thumb brushed against the gentle curve of her breast as he smoothed his hand over her. It stopped at the buckle of her belt, but it only took him a few seconds to loosen the buckle and unsnap the front snap.

Tugging her shirt out of the waistband, he whispered, "You'll be more comfortable without some of your clothes."

"Judd," she said huskily. "This isn't part of our agreement."

"It's hard to keep remembering we aren't supposed to be getting involved when I sleep with you every night."

"The way you say it makes it sound as though we do more than sleep."

"That's probably because I would like to do more than sleep when I'm in bed with you. I'm only human, sweetheart, and I've wanted you since I met you."

His warm hand was under her shirt and gliding over her bare skin, sending shivers of pleasure and need through her. Erin buried her face in his warm neck, biting back a cry of desire. "Go to sleep, Judd."

A shudder shook him as he felt her warm breath

against his skin. Her breasts were pressing against his chest and her slender body was so tantalizingly close to his. He was dying by inches with the need to make love to her, and she expected him to calmly nod off into dreamland.

It wasn't that easy. It hadn't been easy any of the other nights they'd spent together, but he'd managed to put aside his desire for her in exchange for some badly needed sleep.

The last thing he wanted to do at the moment was close his eyes and doze off.

Maybe he could make her want him a little. He would settle for that. For now.

"Erin?" he murmured as he threaded his fingers through her hair.

She made a muffled sound, totally unsatisfactory as a response.

Gently clenching his fingers in her hair, he drew her head back so she was forced to look at him. Her eyes slowly opened, and he felt as though he could drown in the depths of those blue eyes.

He spoke her name as he gazed down at her moist, slightly parted lips, then he kissed her with undisguised hunger. He kissed her thoroughly, intimately, seeking a response and nearly losing his grip on his control when she groaned with aching pleasure.

She was as caught up in the sensual magic between them as he was, he realized with exultation.

His fingers shook as he unbuttoned her shirt. He groaned into her mouth when his hand met no further barriers, and he cupped her bare breast in his hand. His control slipped even further when she arched her back, bringing her hips into his. The feel of her pressing against his hard throbbing length fanned the white-hot fire in his bloodstream.

Easing his hand down between them, he stroked her through the rough material of her jeans. She writhed impatiently, making a whimpering sound deep in her throat. She was so responsive, so utterly desirable, he knew making love with her would be like nothing he'd ever experienced.

Breaking away from her mouth, he nestled his face against her neck, immersed in the scent of her warm, fragrant skin. His hands molded her soft body to his, and he simply held her as he tried to find the strength to stop from taking her completely.

"Judd?"

He shook his head. "It's all right. Just give me a minute."

He was gradually able to loosen his hold on her enough to roll on his back and settle her along his side, his arm keeping her securely locked to him. His fingers combed through her hair as she laid her head on his shoulder. She lifted one hand to his chest, gently stroking.

He laid his hand over hers. "Go to sleep, Erin."

Her voice was quiet, almost a whisper. "I guess this wasn't such a good idea after all. Maybe it would be better if I went back to my room."

His arm tightened around her. Her couldn't let

her go, even though having her in his arms was a sublime torture. "No, it wouldn't be better."

As he waited for his breathing to steady, he listened to the gently crackling sound of the palm fronds blowing in the breeze outside the window. Why had he stopped? he asked himself, without any hope of finding the answer while his body was still pulsating with desire. He knew from her incendiary response to him that she would have accepted his lovemaking, and Lord knows, he certainly was more than willing to lose himself in her warmth.

The fact that there were other people in the cottage didn't inhibit him. The way he was feeling, he would have been able to make love to her in Grand Central Station.

So why had he stopped? The question drummed in his mind with almost as much intensity as his blood throbbed in his veins. Then another question took its place.

What in the hell was happening to him?

After several minutes went by, Erin asked a question similar to the one he'd just asked himself. "What are we getting into, Judd?"

"I think it's safe to say we're involved." His chest rose and fell as he took a deep breath. "I'm certainly not going to complain about getting my money's worth this time."

It was a stupid thing to say, and he realized it when he felt Erin stiffen against him, withdrawing from him even though she remained in his arms.

"Erin, I—"

"Go to sleep, Judd," she said hoarsely. "Don't say anything more. I'll stay only if you go to sleep."

Feeling wrung out, as though he'd been through an emotional wringer, he doubted he would be able to sleep. Regret, frustration, and desire were a potent mixture, and not particularly conducive to sleep.

Because he wanted her to stay with him, though, he dutifully closed his eyes, still holding her tight against him.

# Six

Erin waited. As tired as she'd been when they'd arrived at the cottage, she knew she didn't stand a chance of sleeping now. A few moments ago, she'd been transported to a magically sensual world, only to be cruelly yanked back to harsh reality.

When she felt Judd's arm finally loosen its hold on her, she cautiously raised her head. His breathing was deep and slow, his strong body slack and relaxed.

As carefully as she could, she lifted his hand from her hip and eased away from him. Her shirt parted as she slipped her legs over the side of the bed and stood up. She shivered as she remembered the feel of his hands on her breasts, making it difficult for her to button her shirt.

With one last look at Judd, she walked to the door. She stepped into the hall and closed the door as quietly as possible. Turning around, she nearly bumped into Kate. Dressed in a strapless blue sheath, Kate was carrying a pair of sandals in her hand. Her honey-blond hair was a riot of long curls around her tanned face, and her amber eyes were shining with amusement.

Placing her hand over her heart, Erin exclaimed in a low voice, "Good Lord, Kate. You practically gave me a heart attack. What are you doing up at this hour?"

"I could ask the same thing about you. Roy and I just got home. We went to a movie in Honolulu, then for a long walk on the beach." Kate glanced at the closed door behind Erin. "How about you? Were you tucking in our temporary house guest?"

Erin stepped over to the door of her bedroom. "Good night, Kate."

Kate raised her hands in a placating gesture. "All right. I'll mind my own business. But if it makes any difference, we're all happy for you."

With her hand on the door latch, Erin looked back at Kate. "What are you talking about?"

"Judd. And you. It's about time you realized there's more to life than making money."

"Do me a favor, Kate," Erin said as she swung open her bedroom door. "Don't mention money to me right now, okay? It's not my favorite word at the moment."

"Since when?" Kate asked as she removed one of her dangling earrings. "Making money has been all you've thought about since we opened the doors of the gallery."

Erin frowned at the note of resentment she

detected in Kate's voice. "I thought we all wanted to make the gallery a success."

"We wanted to be successful as artists. Making money wasn't necessarily our priority."

Feeling defensive, Erin explained her own motivations. "It takes money to keep the gallery open so we can display our paintings and hopefully sell them so we can paint more, therefore making us successful as artists. It's also necessary to have a roof over our heads and food to eat. That also takes money."

Kate covered a yawn with her hand. "I thought you didn't like that word."

She would accomplish more by talking to the door, Erin thought. "I'm too tired to argue about this tonight. I'm going to bed."

If Kate said anything more, Erin didn't hear her because she stepped into her bedroom and shut the door.

Even though she was tired and felt as though her brain was wrapped in caramel, she knew she wouldn't be able to sleep. Instead of lying down and at least resting her body, she sat on the cot, thinking about what Kate had said. It was a startling revelation to discover her housemates thought money was all she wanted.

Apparently Judd thought so too.

Well, Judd was wrong, and so were Kate and the others. She considered money only as a means to an end. When she was paid for a work she'd done, she considered the payment a way for her to continue painting. It was proof that what she did was valuable to someone else.

Her lips twisted in a rueful smile. Maybe she was more like her brothers than she thought. Financial success was the only kind of success Michael and the other Callahans understood and recognized. Earning money with her artwork was a way to validate what she wanted to do in their eyes.

Perhaps in her own eyes too. She could have continued to live with Michael on Maui while waiting for Mr. Right to sweep her off her feet, but that wasn't what she wanted. She wanted to earn her own way, to prove she could, to herself and to her brothers.

Her gaze shifted to her closed bedroom door, as though she could see through it and the one beyond, into the other bedroom where Judd lay asleep.

Even though she hated to be considered a money-hungry female, it was just as well Judd thought she was like all the other women who'd taken his money. It made him more cautious about becoming involved with her. She mustn't lose sight of what she was trying to do with her life, and Judd Stafford could make her forget everything simply by touching her.

Since she knew she wouldn't be able to sleep, Erin left her room and went into the studio at the rear of the gallery. Earlier that day, Wayne had left for the island of Hawaii for the weekend. He had a commission to paint a view of the volcano. Even though he wouldn't have expected any conversation if he were there, she was still glad to have the studio to herself.

Erin didn't go to her easel or make any attempt

to work. She knew it would be a waste of time. Still caught up in the enchantment of the moments in Judd's arms, she paced the length of the studio. Somehow she had to forget the magic between them. She had to keep reminding herself he was only going to be on the island for a short time. There was no future for them.

No matter how many times she silently repeated that, though, she couldn't dismiss the fear that her feelings were more than mere physical attraction. She closed her eyes as the truth rocked through her, leaving her shaken and stunned.

She was falling in love with Judd Stafford.

Before she had a chance to get used to the idea, she heard his sleepy voice behind her. "Erin," he said impatiently, "I've been looking all over for you. What in hell are you doing out here?"

She whirled around and saw him standing in the doorway. He'd taken the time to slip on his jeans, leaving the top snap unfastened. His hair was mussed, his eyes drowsy even as he scowled at her.

"Go back to bed, Judd," she said wearily.

"Not without you."

"I want to be alone. I have some thinking to do."

Rubbing a hand over his eyes, he grumbled, "Can't it wait until we get up?"

She shook her head. "This isn't working out, Judd."

He dropped his hand and stared at her. "It would if you'd come back to bed."

"Then what?"

Her quiet question had him rubbing his eyes

again, this time in exasperation. "Then we go to sleep. What else?"

When she turned away from him without answering, he added, "If this is about what happened earlier, I'll promise not to touch you again tonight. Just come back to bed.

"No."

"No?"

She walked over to the rattan couch positioned between the door and one of the easels. Moving aside some of the clutter lying on it, she sat down and leaned back.

"I haven't been doing you any big favor," she said, "by staying with you until you get to sleep. It's solved your problem temporarily, but it isn't helping you in the long run."

He crossed the room and shoved over a jacket and a sketch pad so he could sit down beside her. Sinking onto the cushion, he grunted when one of the springs poked him in the thigh. There was a soft, comfortable bed waiting inside the cottage, he thought irritably, and Erin had chosen a broken-down couch to perch on.

"What's going on, Erin?"

She heard the exhaustion in his voice and almost gave in to his obvious need for more sleep. She resisted. "Instead of just ignoring the problem, we should be figuring out what's causing your inability to sleep, Judd."

"The answer is simple. You left the bedroom."

"I don't mean right now. You're here on vacation because you're having a problem sleeping. If we don't figure out what is causing this problem, you'll still have insomnia when you return to San Francisco."

One of the spokes of rattan stabbed him in the neck when he leaned his head back. Rubbing his neck, he frowned at her. "Do we have to talk about this right now?"

"What better time?"

"One comes to mind, like in a couple of hours from now when the sun is up."

She was about to argue the point when he abruptly stood up and bent down to slide his arms under her. He lifted her off the couch and into his arms.

"Judd, what are you doing?"

"I'm going to bed and so are you," he said roughly. "We'll talk all you want after we both get some sleep."

"This isn't solving anything," she protested, wrapping her arm around his neck as he walked toward the door.

He kissed her briefly. "Are you kidding? It solves a helluva lot. It's the only way I can get you back to bed."

She leaned forward to keep from bumping into the door frame. "I meant your insomnia. Running away from it isn't going to make it go away."

"Maybe not," he said easily as he carried her across the drive toward the house. "Staying awake isn't going to help either."

By the time she'd come up with a response to his statement, he'd pushed open the door of his bedroom. After gently lowering her to the bed, he followed her down and pulled her into his arms. He drew one deep breath, closed his eyes, and fell asleep.

Erin felt her own eyes grow heavy. This was the second battle she'd lost that night. The first was denying her feelings for Judd. She was falling in love with a man who treated her as though she were a handy teddy bear he could take to bed whenever he wanted company while he slept.

Sighing deeply, she closed her eyes.

When she opened her eyes several hours later, Erin was instantly aware of a strange sound. Rolling over, she discovered Judd was no longer beside her. He was standing on the other side of the bed tugging on his jeans.

And he was whistling softly under his breath.

She scowled at him, then rolled back over and pulled the pillow over her head. If she needed any more proof that there was no hope for her and Judd, it was the obvious fact that he was one of those disgusting people who woke up perky and alert, no matter how much sleep he'd had. She, on the other hand, would rather gnaw on leather than have to make conversation before her first cup of coffee.

Judd smiled as his gaze went to the woman in his bed. He finished zipping up his jeans, then walked around the bed to her side. With his hand on her hip, he shifted her over enough to make room for him to sit down.

He shook her hip a little to get her attention. "It's time to get up, sweetheart."

"Go away," she said in a muffled voice.

Chuckling, he changed his tactics. He slid his hand from her hip to her waist. "We have a big day planned which requires you to be standing up and dressed. Those weren't my choices when I woke up with you in my arms, but the plans are already made."

She lowered her hand from the pillow and lifted his away from her waist, then peeked out from beneath the pillow. "What plans?"

He grinned. "It's a surprise."

"I don't like surprises."

"You'll like this one." He ran his finger along her firm jawline. "I'll go get you a cup of coffee while you get dressed."

She batted his hand away. "I am dressed."

"You were dressed. I took off your jeans while you were asleep."

Flipping over onto her back, she looked down at her bare legs, then glared at him. "Why stop there? Why did you leave my shirt on?"

"I admit it was a temptation, but I knew you would really be mad if I took off all your clothes. This way you'll only be half as mad."

"You're the one who's mad. Crazy as a bedbug." She swatted at his hand when he lifted it toward her. "Would you stop touching me?"

"I'd do just about anything for you, sweetheart, but not that. Touching you has become as necessary as breathing."

He stroked her cheek lightly, then stood up. The sight of her tousled hair and slender legs lying atop the white sheet almost made him forget what he'd planned for the day. He'd need little encouragement to change his mind and crawl back into the bed with her. Lord knows, he'd never wanted to leave the bed in the first place. Her shapely body had been warm and desirable pressed against his, and he'd had to use every ounce of control he could muster to keep from waking her with his hands and mouth.

But one of the important things he'd learned in business dealings was that timing and strategy worked better than rushing ahead without thinking things through and possibly blowing the whole deal. This was one battle he planned to win.

"Do you want your coffee before or after your shower?" he asked.

"After," she said firmly. "Then we have to talk. We can't keep going on like this."

He grabbed her hand and pulled her off the bed. When she was standing in front of him, he tugged her against his long frame, his hands sliding down to her silk-covered bottom.

Pressing her to his aching flesh, he said huskily, "No, we can't go on like this. That's why I've made plans for the rest of the day. There are going to be some new rules before we go to bed tonight."

Feeling his hard body against hers destroyed Erin's protests about his making plans without consulting her. All she wanted to do was give in to the storm of feelings he created deep within her. As she tilted her head back to look at him, she told herself she should enjoy his magic while she could. Instead of shutting herself away from him, she should be opening herself up to the joy he brought to her.

It was probably the most foolish thing she would ever do, and a complete reversal of what she'd previously lectured herself to do, but it was what her heart wanted.

Judd accepted her unspoken invitation by lowering his head and kissing her. His tongue surged into her mouth to mate with hers, instinctively seeking the intimacy he was being denied. He'd previously considered himself experienced in the art of lovemaking, but since meeting Erin he was learning there were realms of sensuality he'd never found with any other woman.

Unfortunately, he too quickly reached the point when his heated blood was about to boil over, and loosened his hold on her. As much as he wanted to take her back to bed and give in to the need to make her his completely, he pulled himself back from the brink.

Placing his hands on her shoulders, he spun her around until she faced the door. Then he gently pushed her forward.

"You have ten minutes," he said. "That's about how long it will take me to put everything we need in your van."

Resisting, she raised her hand and placed it on the door frame, stiffening her arm. "I don't know what plans you've made, but you shouldn't have included me in them. I told Kate I would work for her so she could go into Honolulu for some supplies. Then there's the bookwork that needs to be done for the end of the month before I go to the Stafford Building tonight."

Prying her hand away from the door frame, Judd guided her out into the hall. "The supplies Kate needs are being sent out by the art supply store and the books are up-to-date. You now have eight minutes to get ready."

She looked at him over her shoulder, realizing he was completely serious. "You did the books?"

He gave her an exaggerated frown. "I've run a multimillion-dollar company since I was twenty-four, sweetheart. Your set of books wasn't that difficult."

After a short hesitation, she asked quietly, "Why are you doing all this, Judd?"

"It's not that complicated, Erin. I want you to take the day off."

"Even if I don't want one?"

"You need one. You've been working practically every minute since I've known you. If you don't take a break once in a while, you're going to end up a workaholic like me."

"It isn't the same thing."

"It could be. You've been working too hard for too long, just the way I did. I had to be forced into taking a vacation, and now I'm forcing you into taking one day to play."

She shouldn't, but she was actually considering it. He was only asking for one day. Spending the day with Judd would be worth having to work harder later. It might be all she would have before he returned to San Francisco.

She narrowed her gaze. "Has anyone ever told you that you are an extremely pushy man?"

He grinned and nodded. "I believe I have heard that a time or two. The clock is running, sweetheart. What's it going to be? A day of fun in the sun with yours truly at your beck and call, or a day of standing behind the counter in the gallery?"

She couldn't stop her smile. "How much time do I have left for that shower?"

Pleased he was getting his way, Judd reached for her to give her a hug, but as he was pulling her toward him, a man's harsh voice stopped him.

"Get your hands off her!"

Erin and Judd jumped apart and turned to look in the direction the voice had come from, although Judd kept his hand on Erin's arm.

A man built like a bulldozer stood at the end of the hall, glaring at them. There were only inches of space between the man's head and the top of the archway to the hall, and not all that much space on either side.

When Judd didn't release Erin, the man strode toward them. "I said, get your hands off Erin. Now."

Judd let go of Erin, but only after he stepped in front of her, putting himself between the massive man and her. "Who the hell are you?"

Stopping only inches from Judd, the angry man placed his fists on his hips. "I'm the man who's going to pulverize you into little tiny pieces."

Judd felt Erin's hands on his waist trying to move him aside, and he twisted his arm behind him to make her stay where she was. "You look like just the man who could do it," he said calmly. "Would you mind telling me why before you rip my head off?"

The man blinked in surprise. Judd's reaction to his threat was obviously not the one he'd expected.

Erin slipped out of Judd's hold and stepped between the two men. "Patrick, stop it. It's not what you think."

"Dammit, Erin. What the hell do you expect me to do when I find you half-naked with this gigolo pawing you?"

Judd stiffened indignantly. "Gigolo?"

Jerking her head around, Erin gave him a blistering look to silence him. Then she brought her attention back to her brother. "What are you doing here, Patrick?"

"Michael called last night and said I'd better check on you since you hadn't called him since a week ago Friday. I told him I'd talked to you earlier in the week, but you know Michael, he wasn't satisfied until I could report I'd seen you in person and could definitely say you're all right." He glanced at Judd, at her bare legs below the hem of her shirt, then glared accusingly at her. "And it looks like I got here just in time."

Ignoring the rude sound Judd made, Erin faced her brother, anger making her voice quiet and stern. "Don't start, Patrick. I don't need one of your lectures right now."

"You could use one. When Michael hears about this, he's gong to hit the roof."

"No, he won't, because you aren't going to tell him anything other than that I'm fine."

"I just saw you come half-naked out of the bedroom with this guy and I'm not supposed to think there's something going on between you and him?"

"You're going to have to think whatever you like, Patrick. While you're accomplishing that rare event, remember I'm twenty-six years old, not six. Michael promised me I would have time to prove I can manage on my own, so back off. I passed the physical you all insist I take every six months, and Michael has the reports that show I'm perfectly healthy. So you, Michael, Sean, and Shannon have no right to interfere in my life."

Bending down until his nose was only inches from hers, Patrick growled, "Have you slept with this guy, Erin?"

"Yes," she answered without hesitation.

Judd watched in fascination as Erin's brother seemed to swell even larger with indignation and fury. Defusing two hot Irish tempers wasn't going to be easy, but he was going to have to try. Considering Erin's brother outweighed him by at least eighty pounds, stepping between them might not be the smartest thing he'd ever done, but that's what he did.

"Take it easy," he said soothingly. "Erin's sleeping with me, but not the way you think."

"You don't need to explain a thing to him, Judd," Erin said flatly.

He glanced over his shoulder at her. "I have three sisters, Erin. I understand what your brother is feeling. I'd feel murderous, too, if I thought someone was messing around with one of my sisters."

Turning back to Patrick, he explained, "We've slept in the same bed, but I haven't had sex with her. I'm having a little trouble sleeping, and Erin's helping me tackle the problem. That's all."

Erin flinched inwardly as Judd described their relationship in such simple terms. His explanation made her sound like a local sleep remedy. She no longer had to wonder how Judd viewed their relationship.

Patrick studied Judd for a long, tense moment. "We'd better talk." To Erin, he murmured, "Get some clothes on. I'll handle this."

Erin was shaking with anger as she watched Judd follow Patrick down the hall. She didn't know which man she was the most furious with, but it didn't matter. Her anger was enough to extend to both of them. It was bad enough that her brothers treated her as though she needed a keeper. Now Judd was making excuses for her, defending her honor, defusing her brother's temper by explaining a situation that was none of Patrick's or anyone else's business.

Slamming her bedroom door after she's stormed into her room did nothing to quell her fury. A button popped off her shirt as she impatiently tore it off and flung it onto the bed. She yanked open one of her dresser drawers and carelessly sifted through the neatly folded contents until she found what she was looking for.

Judd had arranged for her to have the day off, so she was going to take advantage of it and get far away from him and her brother.

# Seven

The sun was high overhead as Erin walked slowly along the beach, her bare feet sinking into the sand each time she took a step. Waves washed up over her ankles, then receded, only to gather force and return. The constant breeze teased the long fringe of the blue shawl she'd wrapped low on her hips over her bikini bottom and pulled at her unconfined hair.

After two hours of swimming and strolling on the shore of Shark's Cove, her temper had finally dissipated. Oddly enough, once her anger was gone, Erin missed it. She was left feeling empty, with a lingering loneliness that was more difficult to deal with than her anger.

She lifted her face to the sun, absorbing its comforting warmth. She had the cove to herself, her only companions several birds poking their beaks into the sand in search of the tiny creatures burrowed within.

A strand of hair blew across her mouth, and she raised her hand to brush it away. She was startled when warm fingers closed around her wrist.

Jerking her head around, she saw Judd standing only inches away. Dressed in white swimming trunks and a tan and white Hawaiian print shirt, he was wearing dark sunglasses in place of his regular glasses. The wind whipped his hair, the sun highlighting the blond streaks.

He didn't release her wrist.

She pulled her hand free.

After a few moments of silence Erin said, "Since you're still in one piece without any noticeable bruises, you and Patrick evidently had a civilized little chat after I left."

"It was very illuminating."

"I can imagine."

"It took awhile, but I think your brother and I understand each other."

Which was more than she did, she mused.

"For such an understanding man," she asked, "why is it you don't comprehend that I like to fight my own battles with my family? I've had a lot more experience with them than you have."

"You don't have to fight them by yourself any longer."

Not sure how to answer that, she continued her stroll. She wasn't surprised when Judd fell into step beside her. "How did you find me?" she asked, although she thought she already knew the answer.

"Your brother gave me directions to several places he thought you might be that were within

walking distance, since you didn't take your van.
This is the second one I've been to. Is this the one
called Shark's Cove?"

"Yes."

"Charming name for the place you've chosen to
go swimming."

A wave splashed against her thigh. "Do you want
to talk about the geography of the island or get
right to the point?"

"Which point am I supposed to be getting to?"

"The reason you came looking for me. To say
good-bye."

"Good-bye?" He stopped walking and turned her
to face him. "Where am I going?"

She frowned. "How do I know where you'll go?
Back to your shiny condo. To your sister's house.
To San Francisco."

He lifted his free hand to twine a strand of her
hair around his finger. "I'm perfectly happy with
my present accommodations. It's a little more
crowded than I would like, but I'm not planning on
leaving."

She met his gaze unflinchingly. "I think you
should."

"Why?" He smiled. "I have your brother's permission to stay and my rent's paid. Why would I
leave?"

"Because I want you to go."

He removed his sunglasses and slipped them
into the pocket of his shirt. A muscle in his jaw
clenched as he stared down at her.

"Your brother at least gave me a reason why he
wanted me out of your life."

"Which reason did he give you? The threat of bodily harm if you damage so much as a hair on my head, or the one about how delicate my health is?"

"He didn't tell me anything I didn't already know. He said you were a very special woman who deserved only the best life had to offer. I agreed completely. You're going to have to come up with something better than he did to convince me I should leave you alone."

She took a deep breath, then said bluntly. "The reason I want you to go is because I want you to stay."

Stunned, Judd gaped at her. His fingers tightened in her hair, enough to prevent her from moving away, but not enough to hurt her.

"Erin? What are you saying?"

"If you stay," she said quietly and with conviction, "we'll become lovers."

"Would that be so awful?" he asked, his eyes blazing with heat and arousal.

"I could tell you I don't want to make love with you, but we both know that would be a lie. I want you to stay, but it's not that easy. Part of the time, especially when you're touching me, I can convince myself we could simply enjoy each other while you're here. Thousands of people have affairs and accept them as a normal part of life, I tell myself. Living for the moment has a certain appeal, but everything comes with a price. I'm not sure I can pay it once your vacation is over."

Her honesty overwhelmed him, humbled him, yet he was thrilled she'd admitted she wanted him as badly as he'd been wanting her. The least he could do was be equally honest with her.

His hands cupped her face, his fingers threading through her tousled hair. "I could promise you the moon, the stars, and forever, but I don't know what this is between us any more than you do. I'm willing to fight off every one of your brothers for the right to find out what we have going for us, and fight your fears as well. I've never felt like this with any other woman, Erin. I didn't even know something this powerful existed. All I know is I can't walk away from you even if that's what you want me to do."

She raised her hands to clasp his wrists, holding on tightly. "But you will walk away eventually. Your life, your work, your family except for Mrs. Garrison, is in San Francisco."

He didn't want to think about his other life, not when he was touching her. At that moment he was holding his whole world in his hands, and she was all he could think of.

"I'm here with you now," he murmured.

"Are you suggesting I should live for today and worry about tomorrow later?"

He shook his head. "What I'm saying is I'm here now. We're together now. Whatever tomorrow brings will happen then. Whatever happens now is up to us."

Living for the moment had never been Erin's way. Until now. "So what does happen now?"

"Before your brother arrived, we were going to spend the day together. He didn't say anything to make me change my mind."

She felt the muscles in his forearms tighten as he drew her toward him. "You never did tell me what those plans were."

A corner of his mouth lifted slightly. "First, I was going to kiss you."

His breath was warm on her skin. Raising up on her tiptoes, she asked softly, "And then?"

"Then," he murmured against her lips, "we make the world disappear."

The moment his mouth covered hers, the world did disappear. Desire thrummed between them, hot and pulsing and undeniable. The heat of the sun paled in comparison to the flames licking along their veins.

Judd slid his hands over her back, reveling in the feel of her warm, silky skin. Pressing her lower body into his aching loins, he skimmed his lips over her cheek, then her throat. Her taste exploded in his head. When he slipped his foot between hers, his thigh parted her legs. He trembled with the force of his need as the sound of her soft moan penetrated his fogged mind.

He could feel the fringe of her shawl wrap around his thighs as the wind whipped the strands. Her hair brushed across his skin like silken threads binding him to her, even as invisible chains of need linked them irrevocably.

He finally broke the kiss. As he held her clamped against his throbbing body, he sucked badly needed air into his lungs and tried to hang on to his dwindling control.

Then she whispered his name, her voice cracking with emotion.

His control in shreds, Judd drew back from her so he could see her face. Whatever he was looking for he found in the clear, endless depths of her eyes. This wasn't what he'd planned to do when he'd come looking for her. Patrick had implied there were reasons for her brothers to try to protect her, and Judd had decided to find out from Erin what they were. But now all rational thought had been replaced by the grinding need to lose himself in her warmth.

"Open my shirt," he ordered.

Keeping her gaze locked to his, Erin slid her hands up his chest. Her fingers trembling, she slowly worked the buttons free until the wind caught one side of his shirt and whipped it away from his body.

"Now take it off," he said, his voice rough with suppressed desire.

She slid her hands up his chest to his shoulders, then down his arms, pushing the shirt off.

The wind caught it before it fell to the sand and carried it away.

Judd stared into her eyes and saw them shimmer with an incandescent glow as he untied the knot holding her shawl in place. With a twist of his wrist, the shawl flared away from her body like a bullfighter's cape.

He trailed the backs of his fingers along her jawline, down her throat, then tantalizingly slowly to the soft curve of her breast above her bikini top. Smiling into her eyes, he slid a finger under the material and watched in fascination as she closed her eyes and tipped her head back, when his finger brushed across the hard tip of her breast.

He couldn't tear his gaze away from her face. She was so utterly responsive, so compellingly feminine. He had wanted a woman before, but he'd never felt such gut-wrenching need.

When he brought her back into his arms, she stepped onto his feet, giving herself a few added inches and getting closer to him. She lifted her head to meet his descending mouth. Her softness melded into his hardness.

Judd gave his hands the freedom he'd never allowed them before, searching out her delectable curves, savoring her silky skin. He felt her total surrender in the way she responded fully, giving and receiving pleasure with every aching breath.

When his hands swept away the barrier of her bikini top, he held her back from him. He stared, transfixed by the sight of the brilliant sunlight on her naked flesh. She stood in front of him like a pagan princess, her dark hair caressing her skin as the wind tossed the long strands. He found himself envying her hair, wanting to touch her as intimately as it did.

"Erin," he said hoarsely. "You take my breath away."

She lifted her hand and traced her fingers over his jaw, following the same path he'd taken over her skin. When he felt her hand flow across his chest, he groaned, a primitive sound of masculine need, and reached for her.

No matter how close he held her, it wasn't enough. No matter how deeply he kissed her, it wasn't enough. He wasn't sure he would ever be able to get enough of her.

He swung her up into his arms and carried her away from the water toward the palm trees lining the shore. He'd spotted Erin's towel earlier, lying in a small area shielded from the beach by the rough trunk of a palm tree and a few large boulders. The sand was warm under his bare feet even though the spot was in the shade.

He lowered her to her towel, then followed her down. Her mouth was moist from his, her eyes softly alluring as she met his intense gaze.

"If you don't want this," he said hoarsely, "you'll have to say so now, Erin. I've held off as long as I can. I want you very badly."

Even though her arm felt oddly heavy, she raised one hand to his face. "I want this too."

Leaning on his elbow, he lifted his other hand to cover hers, pressing her palm against his cheek. "Are you sure? I can stop now, this minute. It wouldn't be easy, but I could end this if you aren't ready. Once I touch you again, I won't be able to stop."

"Judd," she murmured with a hint of impatience.

He had a stricken look on his face as he gazed down at her. "What? Have you changed your mind?"

She turned her hand to wrap her fingers around his, then brought his hand to her bare breast. "Are you trying to talk me out of making love with you?"

His heart slammed heavily in his chest as he

closed his fingers over her burgeoning flesh. "No! Lord, no."

"Then shut up and make love to me."

His pulse throbbed violently at her words. The heady knowledge that she wanted him swept away the last ounce of his control. He lowered his body onto hers and kissed her with hungry desperation. Her arms came up to capture him, and he had never gone more willingly into the whirlpool of passion.

Now that he knew the waiting had come to an end, he wanted to take his time and savor each delicious second, every atom of sensation. All of his senses were magnified a hundred times over. He could hear her whispering breath, feel her silken skin, and he devoured the sight of her stunning eyes glazed with desire. Her taste lingered on his tongue.

He stroked his fingertips over her face as though his eyes weren't reliable enough. He needed to touch her, absorb her, make her a part of him in every tissue. He drew his hand down her throat to her breast, and his gaze rose to her face when he heard the low sound she made.

"Erin," he said softly. Just her name. It was appropriate for the way she made him feel. Erin had become his whole world.

She responded by saying his name in return as she threaded her fingers through his hair. Her lips were swollen, inviting, her breasts were rising and falling rapidly with the tumult of her breathing.

When she shifted her leg to make room for him,

he thought he would explode with the need to be inside her.

He said her name again, not even trying to hide the aching longing clenching through his body. As his hand swept over her, stroking her thigh and curving hip, he closed his eyes, reveling in the feel of her hips lifting in a provocative movement as old as time.

He took her mouth with deliberate intensity. Her arms twined around his neck. The thrill of being wanted by this incredible woman nearly dissolved his intentions of taking his time with her. The soft yearning sound that vibrated from deep in her throat was nearly his undoing.

"Erin, I'm trying to go slow, but—"

"Don't wait. I—"

This time he finished for her. "I know. It's both pain and pleasure, but it's not enough."

The last barriers of clothing were stripped away before he accepted the invitation of her parted legs. He groaned her name as her warm body accepted him, welcomed him, drew him into a feverish maelstrom of passion. She was incredibly tight around him, incredibly hot.

He wasn't so consumed with desire that he didn't realize he was her first lover. The knowledge stunned him, yet he gloried in the fact that he was the first ever to know her intimately.

Then she arched her hips, and he lost all ability to think. The only reality was the mindless pleasure they found in each other as the surging rhythm escalated, urging them on to the brink of a primitive explosion that eventually consumed them into a fiery void.

Neither was aware of the sound of the waves crashing onto the shore or the breeze flowing over their heated skin. Gradually their breathing slowed and the world righted itself once again.

When he was able to move, Judd rolled onto his back, bringing her with him. He heard her sigh softly as she rested her head in the curve of his shoulder, her breath warm against his throat.

"Are you all right?" he asked, brushing back a strand of damp hair from her cheek.

She made a sound of lazy contentment, and he smiled.

His smile faded as he remembered what had prompted him to ask her the question. "Erin, why didn't you tell me you've never been with a man before?"

"Does it matter?" she mumbled drowsily.

"Only because I would have been more gentle with you if I'd known. I'd have taken more care."

She nuzzled his neck. "I don't have any complaints."

He smiled again and let his hand stroke over the firm line of her spine, smoothing away the particles of sand that were clinging to her skin.

"Any regrets?" he asked.

"No."

"When your brother said you've led a very sheltered life, I didn't realize just how true that was."

His sensitive fingers became aware of a ridge of scar tissue on her lower spine, and he ran a fingertip over it several times. The scar was almost four inches long and half an inch wide. He felt her stiffen as she became aware of what he'd discovered, and he was more curious about her reaction than about what had caused the scar.

"Erin? What happened to you?"

Rather than answer his question, Erin pushed away from him. Sitting up, she glanced around for her bikini, but couldn't see the scraps of material anywhere nearby. Her gaze found his shirt at the base of a palm tree several feet away, where the wind had blown it. If her mind had been on anything other than the question he'd asked, she might have been self-conscious about her nudity. Instead, she shook the sand off his shirt and slipped it on, wrapping it around her body to warm her suddenly chilled skin.

Standing in the shelter of the palm tree, she stared out at the water.

When Judd saw she wasn't going to run away from him, he reached for his bathing trunks and tugged them on. He sensed she would be more receptive to talking to him if he was dressed. As badly as he wanted to go to her, he leaned back against a sun-warmed rock and waited.

It wasn't easy to watch her when his body reacted so powerfully to the sight of her. The wind teased the hem of his shirt, briefly exposing the curve of her naked bottom. His hands burned to run over the tantalizing curves he'd touched only moments before. But there were other things they needed to clear up before he could touch her again.

Finally Erin turned back toward him. She drank in the sight of him. A sliver of sunlight had woven its way through the palm fronds overhead to high-light his hair. The breeze tousled the thick strands, as her fingers had only minutes earlier.

"I thought," she began, "Patrick might have told you about my 'delicate condition.' It wouldn't be the first time my brothers have used my injury as an excuse to discourage men they didn't like."

Judd felt as though the blood had drained from his body, and his relaxed posture was a thing of the past. "What delicate condition? What are you talking about, Erin?" He took several steps toward her, then stopped. "Are you saying there's a phys-ical reason why you shouldn't have given yourself to me?"

Alarmed by the stark terror in his eyes, she quickly walked over to him and laid her hand on his arm. "You didn't harm me, Judd. Sit down, and I'll try to explain."

Feeling his tension, she tugged on his arm to draw him down onto the towel with her. She stroked his forearm in a soothing motion once he was seated and she was kneeling in front of him.

"You didn't hurt me, Judd. I'm perfectly healthy. I have the doctors' certificates to prove it. To ease Michael's mind, I have a complete physical every six months." She shook his arm when he only continued to stare at her, his eyes filled with pain and shock. "I'm telling you the truth."

"Why didn't you tell me you'd been hurt?" he asked in a strangled voice. "I wouldn't have . . ."

She withdrew her hand. "You wouldn't have touched me," she said flatly. "If you'd known about my back injury, you would have treated me as if I were made out of spun glass, the way my brothers do. You would have looked at me the way you are now, as though I will break if you even raise your voice. I suppose I should thank you for letting me feel like a real woman for a little while, even though you'll never touch me again."

She stood and started walking away from him. He caught up with her after she'd taken only a few steps. Clasping her wrist, he whirled her around to face him.

"Dammit, Erin. If you would stop jumping down my throat with accusations and give me a minute to absorb the shock, maybe, just maybe I might surprise you and understand why you feel so defensive."

She met his blazing gaze. Anger had replaced the shock in his eyes. If she'd seen any sign of sympathy or pity, she would have kept walking away from him. She didn't.

"All right," she said heavily. "What do you want to know?"

"Everything, but not just yet. You might have forgotten you're practically naked, but I haven't."

He led her back into the sheltered cove, picking up the pieces of her discarded bikini on the way. Handing them to her, he waited while she dressed. As she lifted one leg to step into the bottom of her bikini, he had to look away. They needed to talk, and seeing her graceful movements only made him want to carry her back down to the sand and make love to her once more.

Out of the corner of his eye, he saw her begin to

slip off his shirt and turned back to her. "Leave the shirt on, Erin."

She met his gaze briefly, then dropped her hands and walked over to the rock he'd leaned against earlier. She sank down on the sand, resting her back against the hard boulder.

He came over and sat beside her, his shoulder brushing hers. He lifted a handful of sand and let it trail through his fingers as he waited.

"I really am all right now, Judd."

Remembering her enthusiastic participation in their lovemaking and the look of ecstasy in her eyes, he said, "I believe you."

"I told you that when I was ten, I was with my parents when a drunk driver hit our car. We were living in Seattle, Washington, at the time. They were killed outright, and I was injured. Along with other problems, I had a spinal fracture."

Judd closed his eyes and leaned his head back against the rock. The thought of her lying in a hospital bed with a broken back left him feeling sick to his stomach. He wasn't aware he'd made a sound until she said his name.

Opening his eyes, he turned his head to meet her concerned gaze. "You've gone this far," he said. "Keep going."

"I would just as soon skip over a few parts. There were long stays in the hospital, a number of operations, and many months of physical therapy before I was classified as well enough to travel to Oahu, where my brothers were living. Michael had been stationed in Pearl Harbor when our parents were killed, and brought Patrick, Shannon, and

Sean here to live with him. He was the oldest and took over the responsibility of raising the rest of us. He hated leaving me in Seattle, but he had to finish his tour of duty here and I couldn't be moved."

"I can imagine how he felt. I hate the idea of your having to go through all that pain alone, and I've only just heard about it."

"Little did I know at the time that getting over a spinal injury was a piece of cake compared to convincing Michael and my other brothers that I wouldn't break into a million pieces if I led a normal life. I managed to go to college as long as I lived with Patrick here on Oahu, even though Michael wanted me to remain on Maui, where he was working for a sugarcane factory. He's the manager of the factory now and still thinks I should return to the island so he can watch every move I make."

"He'll probably always feel that way. Even though my sisters and my mother are married to good men who love them, I still worry about them and hope they're happy. It's not possible for Michael to shut off his protective nature simply because you no longer live under his wing."

After a moment's pause, Erin said quietly, "At least Michael doesn't have problems with insomnia."

Judd frowned at her. "Meaning?"

"You don't have the responsibility of your sisters any longer, and I think you miss it."

"Maybe you're right, but we were talking about your situation, not mine."

"I'm through talking about me. I had a back injury, now I don't. Everything is the way it was a little while ago before you knew about my past."

"I wouldn't say that."

"I knew it," she said heatedly, pushing herself to her feet. "I knew it would make a difference when you found out about my injury. You— What are you doing?"

He'd stood also and grabbed her, tumbling her down onto the sand until she was lying under him. "I'm going to kiss you," he said firmly, gazing into her eyes. "Then Lord knows what will happen after that. The only thing that's changed between us is that I want you more than I did before. Can you live with that?"

She smiled and circled her arms around his neck. "I can live with that."

Even though Erin now knew what waited for her at the end of the tumultuous slide into passion, she was still stunned when Judd slowly slid into her. She barely recognized the eager, demanding creature she became in his arms. But now that she knew that woman existed, the woman who gave pleasure as she was receiving it, she never wanted to return to what she'd been before, only half-alive until Judd had entered her life.

After their heartbeats slowed, she still held him tightly, unwilling to let go of the magic they'd shared, even for a short time.

When he could find the energy to speak, Judd raised his head. Looking down at her, he asked, "Are you all right?"

Her fingers tightened on his bare shoulders.

"Judd, don't do this. Don't make me sorry I told you about my back injury."

His smile was lopsided. "I don't want you to ever be sorry for telling me anything. I'm glad you did tell me. It explains a great deal."

"It does? In what way?"

"Now I know why you're using every moment of every day at the gallery and at your easel. You're making up for lost time."

Erin bit her lip as she thought about what he'd said. His finger stroked her bottom lip to release it from her teeth.

"I never thought about it quite that way before," she said quietly. "You might be right. Just don't start treating me as though I'm a fragile piece of glass."

He caressed her lip again. "It's only that I forgot for a moment to take it easy with you. Once I begin touching you, everything else goes out of my mind." He paused and stared at her. "Why are you looking like that?"

"Like what?"

"Like a sexy kitten who's just lapped up a rich bowl of cream."

"I like the thought that I can make you forget the rest of the world when you're with me."

He eased his weight to one side, keeping her tightly against him. "You do that and more. And you'll have to forgive me if it takes me a while to get over your being injured. I don't like the thought of you hurting or being alone."

Erin didn't like the thought of either one herself, but she knew both conditions were inevitable once

Judd left. Which was why she had to grab for all the memories she could make.

"I've never felt better," she said.

He smoothed his hand over her breast. "I couldn't agree more. You feel fantastic."

"And also very sandy. How do you feel about taking a swim?"

He reached for her bathing suit and handed it to her. "I hate to sound like an old fuddy-duddy, but I draw the line at letting anyone else see you in all your glorious skin."

She in turn found his suit on the sand and gave it to him. "Ditto."

A few minutes later she accepted his outstretched hand and walked beside him toward the ocean.

# *Eight*

Hours later as they came running out of the surf, they both heard the sound of a car door slamming and the unmistakable cadence of excited children's voices.

"It looks like our private cove is about to be invaded," Judd said.

Erin sighed. "Afraid so." It had been a wonderful day full of sun, sea, and passion. She didn't want it to end.

Judd glanced at his watch. Even though he would have liked to have Erin to himself for a little while longer, it was time for them to leave anyway.

Taking her hand, he walked over to where they'd dropped his shirt, her towel, and her shawl on the sand. He scooped them up with his free hand and, drawing her along with him, headed away from the beach.

Erin had to hurry in order to keep up with him. "What's the rush?"

"I didn't realize it was getting so late."

He'd parked her minivan off the road near the path that led down to the water. Before she got in, Erin wrapped the shawl around her hips to protect the upholstery from her wet bathing suit. "Late for what?" she asked.

"We need to get back to the cottage so we can change our clothes." He slid behind the wheel after he folded the towel and placed it on the seat. "Do you know any place nearby where we can get a bottle of wine?"

"The Nabarattis' store about half a mile down the road has wine, but there isn't much of a selection." She grinned at him. "Are you getting tired of Roy's apple cider?"

"We're not eating at home tonight. We're having dinner at your brother's. I don't want to go empty-handed." He chuckled. "A bottle of wine might soften Patrick's aggressive behavior, or I could use it to defend myself."

Erin had been about to climb into the front seat of the minivan, but after his little announcement, she planted her hands on her hips and stared at him. "Since when are we going to Patrick's?"

He reached across the seat and tugged her arm to pull her into the minivan. "Since I accepted his invitation this morning. Come on. We don't have much time. I told Patrick we'd be there by six."

"You shouldn't have told him anything without talking to me first."

"You weren't there at the time." He hooked her seat belt for her. "Before your brother arrived at the cottage this morning, I thought we'd spend the day at the beach, maybe see a few sights, then have dinner at a restaurant in Waikiki. Real food, like a thick steak or a juicy hamburger, instead of seaweed and yogurt. After meeting your brother, I changed our plans."

"I like your original plans better."

He'd known she wouldn't be happy about the arrangements he'd made with Patrick. She was really going to be mad when she heard there was more. He might as well get the rest out of the way.

Keeping his attention on the road, he said casually, "Your brother Michael is going to be there too."

He'd expected some reaction. For her to rant and rave, maybe try to talk him out of going. He really wouldn't have blamed her considering the circumstances. When she didn't say anything, he chanced a glance in her direction. She was staring straight ahead.

"Aren't you going to say anything?"

She shook her head.

Pulling into the driveway, he stopped the van behind the gallery and shut off the engine. He turned in his seat to face her.

"There wasn't time to talk to you about the arrangements for tonight, Erin. Patrick was going to contact Michael this morning after he talked to you. That's when he was going to tell him to hop on a plane and fly over for dinner tonight, so he can see for himself that you're all right and to meet me."

Erin slowly turned her head and met his gaze. "Since there doesn't seem to be anything I can do about Michael coming, I'll see him, but alone. It would be better if you didn't come with me."

"No, it wouldn't. I want to meet your brother."

She smiled faintly. "You've had a small taste of how protective Patrick is. He's a pussycat compared to Michael."

"Patrick and I understand each other. I'm not worried. Why should you be?"

"Because I know Michael and you don't."

He ran his fingers through her hair. "Exactly what are you afraid of, Erin? I'm not going to cause any trouble between you and your brother. I just want to meet him and talk to him. You need someone in your corner. Maybe I can help your brother understand what you're trying to do with your life in a way you can't. I might be able to make things easier between you two."

She choked back a laugh. "You've got to be kidding. Michael has certain ideas about things. You don't fit any of them. Knowing Michael, there's no way he's going to understand our relationship."

Judd tangled a strand of hair around his finger. "I guess we'll just have to make him understand," he said quietly.

Later, when she was in her room changing her clothes, Erin wondered how Judd was going to make Michael understand about their relationship when she didn't understand it herself.

She tucked her white scooped-neck top into the waistband of her rust-colored sarong-style skirt. Considering her top didn't come up to her neck and her skirt barely reached her knees, she knew

Michael was going to lift an eyebrow at her choice of apparel.

After slipping her feet into sandals, she ran her fingers through her hair, debating on putting it up rather than letting if fall around her shoulders. It had been a warm day and it promised to be an even warmer evening at Patrick's. Wearing her hair up would be cooler.

She grimaced. Wearing her hair up or down wouldn't make any difference. It was going to be downright hot at Patrick's no matter how she wore her hair.

Erin was wrong. It was very cool at Patrick's the minute she walked in with Judd beside her.

Patrick and Michael were in the living room. There was no sign of Patrick's wife, Stella, only the two stony-faced Callahans.

As usual, Michael closely examined Erin's appearance, as if with a magnifying glass, as she walked across the room to him. Like Patrick, Michael towered over her as he enclosed her in a hug.

Holding her away from him, he looked down at her, his gaze intent on her face. "Patrick said you were okay. I had to see for myself."

Sighing, she smiled up at him. "As you can see, I'm fine."

He tilted his head to one side. "I'm not so sure. There's something different about you. Something in your eyes I've never seen before."

"It's hunger," she murmured as she stepped back. "I'm starving." She could feel the tension in

Michael as she took his arm, turning him toward Judd to make the introductions.

As the men shook hands, Erin's sister-in-law came into the room. Erin introduced Judd to Stella, who gave him a friendly smile of welcome as she accepted the bottle of wine from him. Glancing around the room, she asked a little too loudly if anyone wanted anything to drink. No one did.

Staring at Judd, Michael jerked his head in the direction of the French doors on his left. Though he raised a brow at the other man's arrogant gesture, Judd followed Erin's oldest brother outside.

Erin groaned and sank down onto the couch. "Well, that was real subtle of Michael, wasn't it?"

Stella collapsed beside her. "Don't say 'subtle' and 'Michael' in the same breath. He was practically breathing fire when he arrived."

Erin frowned at Patrick. "What did you tell him?"

"Exactly what Judd told me to tell him, that it was time for Michael to meet him."

"Judd said that? Why?"

Patrick shrugged. "He's your boyfriend. Ask him."

"He's not my boyfriend."

From long experience of playing the peacemaker, Stella interjected, "Whoever he is, he looks like the type of man who can take care of himself. Erin, I could use your help in the kitchen, and Patrick, you were going to check the steaks that have been marinating for the last four hours."

Erin was happy to keep busy helping Stella in

the kitchen. She nearly sliced her finger instead of a carrot, though, when she looked out the kitchen window and saw Michael smiling. Not a polite, wishy-washy smile, but a genuine expression of mirth.

A little later, she had heard the French doors open, and she walked over to the doorway leading into the living room. Her mouth dropped open when she saw the two men.

Michael was laughing! All Erin could do was stare in amazement. She wasn't alone in that department. Stella and Patrick were standing beside her, as astonished as she, if their expressions were anything to go by.

Judd winked at Erin, showing that he had come away from the meeting fairly unscathed. She would have given a great deal to know what the two men had talked about. Especially when she was undoubtedly the major subject of conversation. Other than that, she could use whatever tactics Judd had come up with in dealing with her brother.

Stella took advantage of Michael's sudden good humor to gather everyone and point them in the direction of the dining room. Erin ended up sitting between Judd and Michael, although she soon began to feel as though she were in the way. The two men kept leaning around her to talk to each other.

When she looked up and met her sister-in-law's gaze, Stella shrugged, as though answering Erin's unspoken question about what in the world was going on. Usually their family gatherings started out with Michael asking Erin about how she was managing on her own. There wasn't an aspect of her life he didn't delve into, including what she was eating, how she was sleeping, and how many hours she was working.

But tonight Michael wasn't asking her any of those questions.

She scooted her chair back a little so Judd and Michael could chat more easily. She listened as Judd explained, in staggering detail, the uses of one of his company's electrical components. His description led to a question from Patrick, followed by a comment from Michael, and the men became even more involved in discussing business.

When Stella served coffee in the living room, Michael finally directed a question in Erin's direction. "How much longer will you be working on the mural in the Stafford Building?"

"It's almost completed. Another couple of nights and I'll have it finished. Why?"

"I was hoping you would be able to take a few days off once you finish that big mural before you start another commission. I'd like you to come to Maui for a weekend soon. From what I hear, you've been working long hours lately and could use some time off."

Erin frowned at Judd before turning her attention back to Michael. "I don't know what you've been told, Michael, but I'm not working any harder than any of my partners."

"I'd still like you to come for a visit while Judd is on vacation. It would give him a chance to see Maui, and give you a break from the gallery."

"Judd can go to Maui without me any time he wants, Michael. I'll fly over with Patrick and Stella for your birthday in two months as usual."

To her amazement, Michael nodded in agreement. Usually when she stood her ground, he argued with her. "I understand your group will be having another open house in a couple of weeks," he said instead. "Will some of your work be on display?"

"Of course."

"I'd like to attend if you'll let me know when it will be."

Instead of answering, Erin got up from her chair and marched over to stand in front of Michael. Holding her hand out, she said, "I'd like to see some identification, please. You look like my brother Michael, but you certainly don't sound like him. What did you do with him?"

For a few seconds there was complete silence in the room. All eyes were on Michael to see what his reaction would be.

To everyone's astonishment—except Judd's—Michael grinned and took her hand in his. "The overprotective ogre is still here, but he's had some good advice from an expert on how to deal with sisters. Especially a sister who's grown up and doesn't need a big brother looking over her shoulder every minute. Apparently it's a common fault of big brothers to be unable to admit their little sisters are capable of making their own decisions and living their own lives."

Erin looked over at Judd, who was watching them with a glimmer of smug satisfaction in his eyes. He was looking exceedingly pleased with himself, and that irritated her. Instead of feeling grateful to him for changing Michael's attitude, she was miffed that the change had taken place because of something Judd had said, rather than as a result of anything she had done. For years she'd tried to convince Michael that she was an adult. Judd had miraculously accomplished that feat in one night.

Still holding on to her hand, Michael got to his feet. "I'm leaving you in good hands. Between Patrick and Judd watching over you, I won't need to worry about you quite so much. As much as I've enjoyed the evening, it's time for me to head back to Maui."

He thanked Stella for the delicious dinner and told Patrick he didn't need to drive him to the airport. He'd accepted Judd's offer to drop him off, since Erin and Judd were going that way anyway.

While Michael was saying good night to Stella and Patrick, Erin drew Judd to one side. "Why did you tell Michael we were going near the airport?" she asked. "It's not on our way home."

"I know, but it's on the way to my condo."

She looked away. She'd know their relationship would end, but she hadn't expected it to be so soon. She walked over to her sister-in-law to thank her for dinner. Of all the surprises the evening had provided, learning Judd was leaving her was the hardest to accept. Still, she was determined to get through the rest of the evening with her pride intact.

Judd watched Erin as she embraced her sister-

in-law and her brother. He thought he was familiar
with all of her expressions, but the shattered look
in her eyes when he'd told her they were going to
his condo was one he'd never seen before.
Granted, the evening hadn't been easy for her, but
he couldn't understand why she suddenly looked
so lost.

Outside, Erin started to get into the back of the
van, but Judd stopped her. "You sit with me.
Michael will sit in back."

"But you'll be dropping me off first," she said. "It
will save having to shuffle around later if I sit in
the back."

He frowned at her. "How do you figure I'm
dropping you off first? We're taking Michael to the
airport, then going to my condo, not the other way
around."

Before she could ask why they were going to his
condo, Michael directed her toward the front seat.
"I have a plane to catch. You two can settle this
later."

The ride to the airport was accomplished
quickly, since Judd had to speed so that Michael
wouldn't miss his flight. Erin had just enough
time to kiss her brother good-bye before he raced
for the gate.

She hadn't even caught her breath when Judd
took her arm and led her back out of the airport.
"Now that we have family obligations out of the
way," he said, "the rest of the night is all ours."

She could have pointed out that there wasn't all
that much left of the night, but she saved her

breath. She didn't have much to spare, considering he was walking so fast.

Once they were back in the minivan, she opened her mouth to speak, but he put his finger across her lips. "Save all those delicious thoughts until we get to the condo. You'll have my complete attention then. I promise."

She snapped her mouth shut, almost clamping her teeth down on his finger in the process. He had a point. She could use a few minutes to gather her thoughts. She had several things she wanted to discuss with him, and it would be a good idea to get them in order before she confronted him.

When they arrived at the building, though, it was difficult to think. As soon as the elevator doors closed, Judd drew her against him, bringing her hand up to his lips. She told herself she was just resting as she leaned against him. It wasn't because her bones were melting or that her heart rate was increasing.

"Judd, we need to talk," she managed to say as his tongue curled around one of her fingers.

"I'm about all talked out, sweetheart. Your brother is one tough nut to crack."

She tugged at her hand. She liked the way he was nibbling on her fingers, but was finding it extremely disconcerting. "That's one of the things we need to talk about. What in the world did you say to him?"

Judd linked his hands behind her, enjoying having her in his arms again. "Using my own experiences with my sisters, I pointed out how holding on to something too tight can strangle it.

It's a viewpoint he's never considered before. I reminded him of what a terrific woman his sister is—emphasis on the word 'woman'—and not a little girl." He moved her away slightly so he could gaze into her eyes. "Sometimes it's difficult to see things clearly when they're right in front of us."

She laid her head on his chest, touched more by the tender tone of his voice than by what he said.

She sighed heavily. "What am I going to do about you, Judd?"

He chuckled. "I have a few suggestions."

The elevator doors opened. He lifted her into his arms and carried her down the hall. A couple of elderly women stared at them, their hands going to their mouths in astonishment.

"Excuse us, ladies," Judd said, smiling at them. "I'm sweeping my lady off her feet."

When he reached his door, he released Erin slowly, keeping her clamped to his side as he slid his key into the lock. Before he opened the door, he said, "Close your eyes."

"What?"

"Close your eyes."

"Why? I can't see where I'm going if I close my eyes."

"That's the whole point." He shook his head in mock exasperation. "Just humor me for a few seconds. Close those beautiful blue eyes."

Throwing her hands up in the air, she did as he asked. "Now what?"

He turned her to face the door, opened it, then pushed her gently over the threshold. He guided her with his hands on her shoulders, then stopped.

"You can open your eyes now."

She did. Then she blinked several times because she didn't believe what she was seeing.

The living room was full of flowers. Not just a few roses in vases, but flowers of every variety in containers of all sizes and shapes on the floor, the tables, the furniture. Plumerias, vanda orchids, bougainvillea, torch ginger, ferns. It was like a tropical paradise.

She slowly turned to him. "I don't know what to say."

He smiled. "A first. Erin Callahan is speechless."

"Except one question."

"I knew it was too good to last. What is your question?"

"Why? Why did you do all this?"

Lifting his hand, he stroked her smooth cheek. "Earlier I had planned on a quiet, intimate dinner here with just the two of us. Real honest-to-goodness food. Not a single bite that could be classified as health food."

She smiled at his reference to Roy's cooking. Her smile faded as he picked up a plumeria blossom from a table and brushed it across her lips.

"When our dinner plans were changed, I canceled the caterer."

"But not the florist."

He shook his head, his gaze on the soft petal against her skin. "I didn't want to cancel the flowers. They're an important part of a fantasy I've been having lately."

"I didn't realize you were the kind of man who had fantasies."

He tucked the plumeria blossom behind her ear, then grasped her shoulders. "This is the first since I was fourteen and I had a fantasy about the overdeveloped cheerleader who lived next door. Nothing came of that fantasy. Lately, I've had this fantasy about making love to you in a field of flowers. Since this is a crowded island with lots of wandering tourists, making love to you outside might get us arrested. This seemed like the next best thing. And I'm determined to make this fantasy come true."

She smiled. "What can I do to help you with it?"

He drew her down with him onto the flower-covered carpet. "You are my fantasy."

Her body crushed the flowers beneath her, releasing their strong, sensual fragrance. She looked up at him as he partially covered her body with his.

"I'm not a fantasy, Judd. I'm very real."

He stroked his hand over her waist and hip, shaping her gentle curves. "So is the way you make me feel. Like every nerve ending is alive, like I'll explode if I can't bury myself inside you."

She lifted her hand to cup the side of his face. Desire glowed clearly in his eyes. It was an expression she would never forget.

"What was I doing in this fantasy of yours? I want to do my part."

Propping himself up on one elbow, he tugged on her shirt. "For one thing, you weren't wearing this."

Keeping her gaze locked to his, she sat up, then pulled the shirt off over her head. She smiled when she heard him inhale sharply. She wore nothing under the shirt.

His hand slid over her waist toward her breast. She guided it instead to the fastener of her skirt. "What about this?"

"It has to go too."

With a few deft moves, he had the skirt loosened and drawn down her legs, then swept her panties away as well. For a moment, he devoured the sight of her naked body lying on a cushion of colorful blossoms.

"Erin, you are the most exquisite woman."

With the pressure of her hand behind his neck, she brought his face down to hers. "Kiss me."

He groaned as he complied with her request, willingly taking everything she offered. His head was swimming with the explosion of his senses. Anticipation had him hard and aching.

He broke away from her mouth when he felt her hand spread across his rib cage and slide down to the fastening of his jeans. He clasped his fingers around her wrist to stop her.

"Not yet. I want this to last longer."

She shook her head. Her breathing was ragged as she whispered, "I don't think I'll last. I want you now."

Resenting the time it took to remove his clothes, he tore off his shirt and jeans, his gaze never leaving her face.

Then he came down to her, covering her with his

heated length. When she closed her eyes, he murmured, "No. Look at me."

Slowly, she raised her lashes and met his blazing gaze. When she lifted her hips, he couldn't hold off any longer. He slid into her warm, welcoming body, taking her soft moan into his mouth as he kissed her.

As he knew it would, the world disappeared, leaving only the two of them.

# Nine

After the magical night spent with Judd in his condo, Erin had to drag herself back to reality when they returned to the cottage the following day. There was a message for Judd to call his sister at Stafford Industries as soon as possible, and Erin was hit with the news that there was no hot water in the cottage.

Judd used the phone first while Erin looked through the phone book for a plumber. After he finished his call, he sat down beside her at the kitchen table.

"Justine needs to see me," he said. "There's some family problem she won't discuss over the phone, so I'm going to have to go to the office this morning. I'll take your van if you don't need it, or I can have the company limo pick me up."

"I don't need the van until tonight," she said, still scanning the list of plumbers. "You can use it as long as I have it back by six."

He glanced down at the phone book. "Do you want me to take care of getting a plumber before I go?"

She jotted down a couple of phone numbers on a pad of paper. "I'll handle it. It isn't the first time we've had a plumbing problem. Rustic charm has its drawbacks. The trick is getting in touch with a plumber who will come out immediately instead of a week from today."

She could have added that she was hoping to find one who wouldn't want an arm and a leg plus a large chunk of their profits. The bank account of the gallery wasn't in the red, but it wasn't exactly in the black either. More of a light gray.

Judd drew her up from the chair and into his arms. "This isn't how I wanted to spend the day," he murmured against her neck.

She closed her eyes as she absorbed the feel of his hard body pressed against hers. She wanted to soak up as many sensations as she could.

"Sometimes we can't always have what we want," she said quietly.

Lifting his head, he looked down at her. "Sometimes we can."

She knew what to expect when he then kissed her. The explosion of her senses was familiar, yet new, making her wonder if she would ever take the effect Judd had on her for granted. Her arms came up around his neck to hold him closer. She wanted to hold on to her little piece of heaven before she was dashed back to lonely reality.

Judd felt her response in every fiber of his being. One of the hardest things he'd ever done was to pull away from her instead of carrying her off to his bedroom.

"As much as I would like to continue this, I have to leave," he muttered. "If I kiss you again, I won't be able to stop."

With great effort, she stepped back. "I'll get my keys for the van."

Judd leaned against the counter after she left the kitchen. He was glad of the few minutes to try to make some sense out of her reactions. There'd been an almost desperate quality to her kiss just now, then she'd seemed to withdraw, not just physically, but inwardly. He couldn't understand why. As much as he hated to leave her, going to the office would give him a chance to put a few things in motion. He probably should have contacted Justine earlier once he'd decided exactly what he wanted to do.

But for the last couple of days, all he had thought about was Erin.

He smiled. It was an affliction he was going to suffer from for a very long time. Like the rest of his life.

When she returned, she handed him the keys. "Remember, I'll need my van back by six."

"No problem. I'll be back in plenty of time. What are you going to be doing other than deal with the plumbing while I'm being hassled by my sister?"

"I'll work in the studio. I have a few more paintings I want to finish before the open house."

He pulled her into his arms again. "Will you be okay while I'm gone?"

She knew he only meant today, and she also

knew she wouldn't be okay once he was gone for good. "I'll be fine."

He allowed himself one more taste of her mouth before he left. The quicker he got to the office and took care of business, the sooner he could return.

Judd had been gone for thirty minutes before Erin finally found a plumber who would come out that afternoon. Every other one she'd called had offered excuses, evasions, and promises for "some time" that week. Hoping that the last one she'd called would actually arrive that afternoon as he'd guaranteed, she jotted down the company's name and number.

She was putting the phone book back in the drawer when Roy walked in the back door. "Any luck finding a plumber?"

"I think so. There was only a couple left to call when I finally got one who said he'll be out this afternoon."

"Good." Roy lingered by the door rather than coming into the territory that was normally exclusively his. "Ah, Erin. Do you have a minute?"

"Sure. What's up?"

"I hate to pile on even more problems for you, but the last couple of days you've been occupied with Judd, so we haven't had a chance to tell you our news until now. I'm afraid it can't wait."

"What is it?" she asked, puzzled.

Roy walked over to the table and sat down. "Sit down, Erin."

She was liking this less and less. Whatever Roy wanted to tell her, it didn't sound like good news. This seemed to be the day for it.

Pulling out a chair across from him, she sat. "If your stove in on the blink, this is the day to announce it."

He stared down at the table, playing with the narrow fringe on the placemat in front of him. "No. It's nothing like that."

She waited for him to say more. When he didn't, she asked, "Then what is it, Roy?"

"I guess there isn't any way to say this other than just blurting it out."

"That would be nice. So blurt."

"Kate and I are moving out."

Erin sat back. "If it's about the lack of hot water, I'm getting that fixed."

He leaned toward her, resting his forearms on the table. "It isn't because of the plumbing," he said earnestly. "It's the lack of privacy. Kate and I have been thinking about finding a place of our own for about six months. We started seriously looking for vacant rentals in the area about a month ago, when she thought she might be pregnant. After visiting the doctor a couple of days ago and finding out she is pregnant, we decided we can't put off moving into a bigger place. The husband of one of the nurses in Kate's doctor's office is getting a transfer, and they want to rent their house. We're going to go look at it this afternoon."

Erin jumped out of her chair and hurried around the table to hug him. "That's wonderful news!"

He hugged her back, then stared at her. "That's not the reaction we thought we'd get. To be honest, we thought you'd be upset about us moving out."

Stepping back, she gaped at him. "Are you serious? I'm happy for you and Kate. You're going to have a baby. That's terrific."

"But, Erin, what about the rent on the cottage? We'll still share the expenses of the gallery, but we won't be able to pay our part of the rent once we move into our own place."

She placed her hands on her hips and frowned. "Don't tell me you think all I care about is money too? We've been friends a long time, Roy. I thought you and Kate knew me better than to think I would put money ahead of your happiness."

"It's not that, but how will you manage to keep the cottage on your own? With Polly gone, Wayne staying on Maui for several weeks, Judd returning to San Francisco, and now Kate and I moving out, what will you do?"

She placed her hand on his arm. "Don't worry about me. You have a wife and a child to think of, and they have to come first. We'll keep the gallery going one way or the other."

He looked away, then back at her. "We . . . ah, thought maybe you and Judd . . ."

She shook her head, smiling faintly. "Judd will be going back to San Francisco in a couple of days, and I'll be staying here."

After a pause, Roy said gently, "I'm sorry, Erin. Everyone seems to be walking out on you."

"That's just the way things are working out. I believe that's what is called life. When we first began making plans for the gallery, we all knew we were going to have to make a lot of adjustments. It would be unrealistic to think we would all be living together for the rest of our lives." ·

"It's just that you've been the major force in getting the gallery established and keeping it going. We've left so much up to you, which hasn't been fair. Judd pointed that out to us. We've taken advantage of you, and you've done a sensational job. Now we're all abandoning you."

Unsure how much longer she would be able to keep up her casual attitude, she took his arm and led him out of the kitchen. "Let's go find Kate. After I give her my congratulations about the baby, I'm going to suggest she start packing up her mobiles and wind chimes immediately. She might just finish by the time you move into your new house."

It took Judd longer than he'd expected, but he accomplished a great deal during his day at the office. When he returned to the gallery, he couldn't park in the usual spot. It was taken up by a large blue van with the logo of a plumbing firm in white letters on the side. Erin was standing near the driver's door saying something to the man behind the wheel.

Judd remained in the minivan for a minute enjoying the sight of the sun glittering off her dark hair, the wind tossing it about her shoulders. He'd been away from her for about five hours, yet he felt as though he hadn't seen her for days. The thought of having to leave her even for a short time was painful.

But that was what he had to do. When he'd left that morning, he hadn't expected to have to make plans to leave the island that same day.

After the plumber left, Judd got out of the minivan and started walking toward Erin. She stood still, waiting for him. The sight of her at that moment was one of the pictures he would take with him, so that he could remember her during the lonely nights without her.

He stopped only inches from her and cupped his hand at the back of her neck, then lowered his head and briefly kissed her.

When he raised his head and looked down at her, the strange expression on her face surprised him. Sadness and pain were mixed with pleasure and the warmth he'd come to expect from her.

Before he could speak, her gaze shifted to something behind him. Glancing back to see what had caught her attention, he saw the company limousine glide to a stop behind the minivan.

He turned back to Erin and opened his mouth to explain, then paused at the look of resignation in her eyes. He got the impression she knew what he was going to say.

"I have to leave for San Francisco right away," he said bluntly.

He thought he saw her flinch, then figured he must have been mistaken when she calmly said, "All right."

She stepped aside to clear his way to the door of the cottage. "I suppose you'll want to pack."

Her voice was flatly polite without any of the warmth he'd become addicted to receiving from her. "I didn't come for my clothes. I don't need them. I came back to tell you why I have to leave sooner than I planned."

"You could have phoned. You don't owe me any explanations, Judd. I knew you would be leaving the island eventually."

His gaze drilled into her. He'd expected her to be upset that he was leaving, perhaps even angry at the short notice. He hadn't expected her blank acceptance.

"If there were any other way," he said, "I would have taken it."

She lowered her gaze. "I know."

He fought back the anger rising in him. Losing his temper wouldn't accomplish anything. Patience might.

When she turned toward the cottage, he clenched his hands to keep from grabbing her and shaking some sense into her. Then he saw the rigid way she was walking, her spine straight, her usually graceful stride stiff and awkward. She wasn't as cool and unconcerned about his leaving as she wanted him to believe. Following that thought was another. He sensed she wanted to send him off with a casual farewell and no tears, recriminations, or regrets.

Catching up with her in the hall, he took a hold of her arm and turned her around to face him. "Dammit, Erin. I don't want to leave, but I have to. My sister and brother-in-law are going away on vacation, and Sam wants to check me over again before they leave so he can reassure my family that I'm fine."

"I understand, Judd."

Releasing her, he slid his hand into the back pocket of his jeans and drew out his wallet. Her sudden gasp had him raising his gaze to hers. She'd gone incredibly pale, staring at the wallet with what could only be classified as horror.

"If you offer me money," she said tightly, her gaze still fixed on his wallet, "I'll never forgive you."

He raised a brow at the sharp tone of her voice. "I wasn't going to give you any money."

He opened the wallet and withdrew a white card. Extending it to her, he said, "This is my business card. I've written my home number on the back. I hope to get a flight back here in a couple of days, a week at the most. I won't know until I get there how long it will take me to clear up things at that end. If you need me for anything, I can be reached at any of these numbers."

Her hand came up almost in slow motion to take the card from him. For several seconds she simply stared at it, then she turned it over to read the number he'd written on the back. She seemed to be gauging every move she made very carefully.

Her reaction puzzled him. He couldn't pin down what exactly was wrong, but something definitely was.

He spoke his thoughts aloud. "I wish I had more time to spend with you before I go, but the faster I get back to San Francisco, the sooner I'll be able to return here."

She started down the hall, then stopped and

came back to him. "I forgot. You said you didn't need your clothes."

He cupped her face in his hands to keep her in front of him. "I have time enough for a proper good-bye kiss."

She lifted her chin and gave him a small smile. "The proper farewell in the islands is to present the traveler with a lei and a kiss. If you'd given me a little more warning, I would have made one for you."

"I'll settle for the kiss."

He slowly pulled her to him, drawing out the pleasure as long as he could. It was going to have to last him awhile. Then he kissed her deeply, hungrily. The thought of not being able to kiss her, touch her, love her while he was gone was like a cavern of emptiness he tried to fill with her taste.

Drawing back from her while he still could, he trailed his finger over her jaw. "Damn, I don't want to leave you."

His gaze was drawn to her lips as she licked them, as though savoring the taste he'd left there. He groaned. "I wish I had more time."

"But you don't. Your car is waiting."

Slipping his arm around her waist, he felt the tension in her body. "Are you okay?"

"Sure," she said breezily. "Why wouldn't I be?"

He pushed open the screen door, then looked down at her. If she held herself any stiffer, she would snap in two, he thought. "Did you have trouble with the plumber? Didn't he take care of the problem?"

"He put in a new hot water heater."

"Good. Lord knows I'm going to be taking plenty of cold showers once I get back to San Francisco. I would hate to think of you taking them as well."

The chauffeur opened the door for Judd as they approached the limousine. "We have thirty minutes before your flight leaves, Mr. Stafford."

"I know." Resting his hand on the top frame of the door, he leaned down and kissed her. "I'll call you."

Erin remained standing in the gallery parking lot long after the long gray limousine had disappeared down the road.

He'd been so happy, she mused, so excited to be returning to San Francisco, even though it meant leaving her behind. Each of his words had grated against her raw nerve endings like fingernails on a blackboard.

Eventually she started toward the back door of the gallery. She had to do something. Otherwise she would begin feeling incredibly sorry for herself, and that wouldn't accomplish anything. What she should be doing, she told herself, was finding a way to pay the plumber's bill. Who would have thought one little hot water heater could cost as much as one of her paintings?

She kicked a piece of gravel, then yelped and bent down to hold her sore bare toe. Next time she kicked something hard, she should remember she was wearing sandals and not shoes.

But a sore toe was nothing compared to the ache in her heart.

She quickened her step. No, she would not feel sorry for herself. She'd gone into the relationship with Judd with her eyes wide open. She'd also foolishly opened her heart and let him walk in, but she would live. She'd survived one crash in her life. She would survive this one too.

She walked through the gallery to the front door and took down the Closed sign. It had been necessary to close the gallery while the plumber was at the cottage, since Roy and Kate had gone to look at the house they wanted to rent.

Returning to the counter, she got out the business directory, where she kept phone numbers and addresses of current and potential clients.

Twenty minutes later she hung up the phone and jotted down the order she'd been given. One hundred paintings of a pineapple and fifty paintings of Diamond Head, all five by seven inches and framed, to be delivered in two weeks. If they sold well, she would have repeat orders. That would cover the hot water heater, and she'd have a little left over to apply toward the rent. She breathed a sigh of relief that the gift shop had still been interested in having her fill their order, even though she'd turned them down several months ago.

By the time Kate and Roy returned from looking at the house, Erin could honestly tell them their moving out wouldn't cause her any problems with the rent.

She wasn't going to be living at the cottage either.

# Ten

Judd paced the length of his office. It took him exactly seventeen steps to get from one end to the other. He was surprised the expensive carpet did not yet show any signs of the extreme abuse it had been getting during the last couple of hours.

Suddenly he stopped, turned, and strode to his door. Yanking it open, he yelled, "Fiona! Get in here."

He resumed his pacing, changing his route from the door to his desk and back. He was near his desk when the soft, controlled voice of his secretary came from the door.

"You roared?"

He whirled to face her. "Have you made those plane reservations for Hawaii yet?"

The gray-haired woman adjusted her spectacles on her nose. "There's a flight departing at nine o'clock tomorrow morning."

"You couldn't get anything sooner?"

"I could if you wanted to charter a plane. If you want a commercial flight, you take the one tomorrow morning."

He sat on the edge of his desk. "See what you can do about chartering a plane. I'll go crazy if I have to wait one more day. It's been two long weeks since I left, and I've only talked to Erin once in that whole time and then only for a few unsatisfactory minutes. I have to get back and find out what in the hell is going on."

Fiona McDaniels stepped into the office. "Since you've waited this long, one more day won't make that much difference. Your mother is expecting you tonight and would be terribly disappointed if you missed your own farewell dinner."

Sighing heavily, Judd crossed his arms over his chest. "I forgot about that damn dinner."

"It's your mother's wish to have the whole family together one last time before you leave for Hawaii. Mrs. Garrison and her husband have flown here especially for this evening, and Dr. and Mrs. Sampson have cut their vacation short in order to be here too."

He held up his hand. "I get the picture, Fiona. I'll take the morning flight."

Fiona sat in one of the chairs facing his desk. "I thought you might. I already made your reservation." She slipped off her shoes and stretched her feet out on the carpet. "I'm bushed. You've really been cracking the whip the last two weeks, boss. I didn't think we'd get it all done in the time frame you were allowing."

Judd grinned at his secretary. "You'll love Hawaii, Fiona. Aside from the fact that I would have a difficult time finding a secretary who would put up with me the way you do, you won't regret making the decision to move to Hawaii."

"I still don't think it's right I move into the company condominium, though. It doesn't sound like my style."

"It's only temporary, until we find you a place of your own. You need someplace to stay, and I need you there to help me make the transition go smoothly." He frowned. "Evidently I'm going to have my hands full trying to find Miss Erin Callahan."

"From what you've told me, she's busy with her business."

"Then why doesn't she answer the phone in the gallery? All I get from Kate are evasions and excuses. She keeps telling me she's given Erin all my messages, but Erin hasn't called me back. Not once. She doesn't answer the phone at the cottage either. Even at night when she should be there. Justine said the mural in the lobby was finished two days after I left, so Erin should be in the cottage at night. I phoned her brother Patrick, and he told me he saw Erin last Friday. According to him, she looked a little tired but otherwise was fine, and was apparently really busy with her work."

"Why is that so hard for you to believe?" Fiona asked. "You said yourself she is committed to making the gallery a success. Of all the people who should understand someone working hard, it should be you."

He began pacing again. "I understand why Erin's working so hard. I know how important her painting is to her. What I don't understand is why she isn't returning any of my calls. It makes me wonder how important I am to her."

Fiona slipped her feet back into her shoes and stood. "I can't help you there, since I've never met her. However, I've gotten a clear picture of how important she is to you. I don't know any other man who would move his business and his home to another state for a woman he's known only a couple of weeks. Especially a man who has repeatedly said he was never going to get tied to a woman."

Judd stopped pacing. "You're enjoying this as much as Sam is, aren't you?" he said accusingly. "Old Judd is getting his previous words crammed down his throat."

Fiona shook her head. "I'm not laughing at you, Judd. And I don't think Sam or anyone else in your family is either. We're happy for you. You have to admit, though, that you've had an abrupt change in attitude in a very short time."

He grinned. "When you're hit with a lightning bolt, it tends to change your attitude."

"I can hardly wait to meet this woman. I've never met a lightning bolt before."

A determined glint entered Judd's eyes. "This is one lightning bolt who is going to be grounded. If I can ever find her."

He thought about the one time he'd talked to

Erin since he'd left the island. She'd asked him about his checkup, then said she was glad he'd been pronounced in good health. When he added he'd been sleeping all right, her reaction had been one of stilted pleasure.

The short call had been totally frustrating, barely better than not talking to her at all.

He kept remembering the haunted expression in her eyes just before he'd left her. Now he wished he'd insisted she come back with him to San Francisco. This separation was harder than he'd expected. Being without her was forcing him to push himself and everyone else harder to get everything settled faster so he could get back to her.


Erin opened her eyes. Instead of the familiar ceiling of her bedroom, she saw blue sky and palm fronds. She groaned softly. She'd fallen asleep. This was the first afternoon she'd taken off in what seemed like forever, and she'd spent part of it sleeping.

She ran her fingers through her windblown hair, pushing it back away from her face, as she stood up. Brushing the sand off her legs, she began to walk toward the water. Waves were crashing onto the shore a little higher than normal due to an offshore storm the previous night.

As she stared out across the water, she thought about the past couple of weeks. She'd finally finished the order for the gift shop, and with the money she'd earned, she'd paid the plumbing bill.

Roy and Kate had moved out, leaving the cottage looking bare with all the wind chimes gone. Though the place seemed almost hauntingly empty now that she was the sole occupant, she knew it still was going to be difficult to leave when the owner found someone to buy it.

Receiving the notice that the owner wanted to sell the cottage couldn't have come at a worse time. No matter how she had tried to find a way to purchase the cottage herself, her finances just wouldn't cooperate. Her share of the profits from the gallery wasn't enough for her to qualify. Even with the additional income from the gift shop orders and the commission she'd recently taken to paint a series of three paintings for an insurance company, she couldn't meet the bank's requirements.

She could understand the bank's position. Her line of work didn't provide her with a dependable weekly income. Some months were better than others, but she couldn't guarantee the set amount of income the loan officer insisted on.

She leaned down and picked up a shell, turning it over and over in her hand. She should be out looking for an apartment instead of dithering away precious time wandering around the beach.

Thinking of Judd.

As the surf slid up the sand and covered her ankles, she dropped the shell into the water. She had spent too much valuable time thinking about Judd. All she had were memories, and they were a poor substitute. Hearing his voice the one time she had been home when he'd called had nearly killed her. He'd been teasing, impatient, and loving, and she missed him so badly, she couldn't bear to hear his voice again. She took the messages from Kate that he had called, but couldn't make herself phone him back. Soon he would resume his life and forget about her. At least she hoped it would be soon. Every time Kate told her Judd had phoned, her heart twisted painfully, the temptation to hear his voice one more time fighting her determination to forget him.

Apparently her strategy was working. Judd hadn't phoned in three days.

Coming to Shark's Cove hadn't been a good idea, though, she thought. There were too many vivid memories of the day they had spent there.

She glanced toward the small sheltered spot where they had made love, then blinked. Now her imagination was playing tricks on her. She could almost see him leaning against the rock where he'd stood before. The wind was tousling his sun-streaked hair, just as it had then.

She blinked again. But he hadn't been wearing a suit that day. Why in the world would she imagine him wearing a suit? she wondered in astonishment. A mind was a precious thing to waste, and she had lost hers.

Then the vision moved. It was actually walking toward her, coming closer and closer.

A strong wave splashed against her legs, soaking the lower half of her white denim skirt. She took a step in the direction of the mirage, then stopped. He seemed so real.

"You're a hard lady to find."

She stared. He was real. Just to make sure, she stammered, "Ju-Judd?"

"So you remember my name. That's encouraging."

She raised her hand slowly and touched his chest. He was warm, hard, and solid. "I don't believe this. What are you doing here?"

"I came looking for this woman I met when I was in the Islands a couple of weeks ago. She was a beautiful, sensual, exciting woman who was also the most honest lady I've ever known."

"Why did you come looking for her?" she asked. Since she'd been holding her breath, she was surprised she could even speak.

Hope was a frail seed that had been dormant for weeks and was beginning to break through the hard shell encasing it.

He didn't answer her question. Instead he asked her, "Why didn't you respond to any of my messages?"

"I wasn't sure what the point would be. You were in San Francisco and I was here. You were busy with your work and I was busy with mine."

"That's it? You can dismiss what we had, can still have, so easily?"

"Judd," she said carefully, "what else am I supposed to say? How can we have anything else considering you live five hours away by plane?"

He stared at her long and hard. "You didn't think I would return, did you?" he asked, a note of disbelief in his voice.

The sun was glinting off his glasses, and she couldn't see his eyes. "No, I didn't."

He whirled around and took two steps away, then turned back to her. "Have I been so besotted with you that I saw only what I wanted to see in our relationship? I can't believe I was so wrong about us, Erin. I won't believe you think what we had was just a temporary vacation affair."

"What else am I supposed to think? One minute you were here, the next you were on a plane back to San Francisco. Your headquarters, your family, your home is there, not here. Is this what you plan to do, just pop in and out of my life like this? I didn't even know you were arriving today."

"That's because you don't answer your phone or return my calls. If you had, I would have told you I'm in the process of moving my headquarters to Honolulu so we can be together."

"Wh-what?"

Ignoring her question, he went on. "If you'd bothered to talk to me, I would have known Kate and Roy had moved out of the cottage, that the cottage was being sold out from under you, and that you've been working yourself into the ground trying to keep everything going. Instead I had to find all this out from Kate when I went to the gallery looking for you. If you had told me, I would have told you not to worry about money. I'll give you whatever you need."

"I don't want your money," she said flatly.

"Or my help, apparently. You didn't even think of asking for my help, did you?"

"So you could offer me money? I know that's what you expect from women. You've made that clear. I'm not like that."

"That was in the beginning. Not after I got to know you better."

"And how well do you know me, Judd? We were together less than two weeks. That's not all that long."

He stared intently at her. "It was long enough for me to fall in love with you. I guess my mistake was in thinking you felt the same way about me."

Erin's heart thudded heavily, painfully, in her chest. "You love me?"

"Of course I love you, you nitwit. What the hell do you think all this is about? I don't change my whole life for someone who's a nodding acquaintance."

"You never told me you loved me before you left."

"I told you how I felt every time I made love to you. I don't think I could have been clearer if I'd put it on the front page of every newspaper from here to China."

She took a step toward him, joy and happiness exploding within her, but he held up his hand to stop her from coming closer. "No. If I touch you, I'll convince myself that just having you in my arms again is enough. It's not. I want your love and trust, Erin. Apparently, at the moment I don't have either. Maybe you're right. Maybe you need more time. If that's what you want, you got it."

Erin couldn't move. She couldn't find her voice to call him back. Shock kept her rooted to the spot as he walked away.

Erin stood in front of the door of Judd's condominium and placed her hand on her stomach, where a flock of butterflies had taken up residence. She started to knock on the door, then hesitated. Biting her lip, she told herself to carry through with it. There was too much on the line for her to chicken out now.

Taking a deep breath, she raised her hand and rapped her knuckles several times on the door. She waited for what seemed like hours and knocked again, a little harder.

She frowned when she heard a muffled sound on the other side of the door. Her frown deepened when she realized it was a woman's voice. And unless her hearing had been badly affected by her sleepless night, the voice didn't belong to Judd's sister.

She turned away from the door. Whoever the woman was, Erin didn't want to see her. Especially if Judd was there also.

She had reached the elevator and was about to press the button when she heard the door open. Against her will, she looked back.

A gray-haired woman wearing a bulky chenille robe was standing in the open doorway staring at her. "Erin Callahan?"

"Yes," Erin answered hesitantly.

Extending her hand toward Erin, the older woman said, "Come in, come in. I just made a fresh pot of coffee."

Erin started walking toward her. "I don't mean to be rude, but I don't know who you are."

Keeping her right hand out in front of her, the older woman grinned. "I'm Fiona McDaniels, Judd's private secretary. And it's *Miss* McDaniels, due to an unfortunate lack of discerning men who prefer brains to beauty."

Erin shook her hand. "I'm pleased to meet you, Miss McDaniels. I thought Judd would be here."

Fiona took her arm and drew her into the living room. "He's not staying here. He's given me the condo to use until I find a place of my own. Please sit down. Make yourself as comfortable as you can in this furniture showroom. I'll bring in the coffee."

A few minutes later Erin accepted a cup of coffee from Fiona. "I'm sorry for arriving so early. I've obviously disturbed you."

"Nonsense. Very little disturbs me except obnoxious salesmen who won't take no for an answer." Fiona sat on the couch and thoroughly studied Erin. "You do interest me though. I've been wanting to meet you since Judd first told me about you when he came back from his vacation. I was hoping I could meet the lightning bolt that struck him down."

"Lightning bolt?"

"That was his word for what happened to him. I think it fits. Having worked for him for eight years, I've seen him in a variety of different moods. It was quite a revelation to see him knocked off his feet."

"He's not the only one who's been knocked off balance," Erin murmured.

For a moment, Fiona didn't comment. She sipped her coffee and continued to examine Erin with a frank gaze. At last, she leaned over and patted Erin's hand. "I'm pleased to hear that. I always thought when Judd fell, he would fall hard, and I'm happy to say it looks like I was right."

"Do you know where he is, Miss McDaniels? I really need to talk to him."

Fiona glanced at her small wristwatch. "He said he was spending the night at his sister's house, but if I know him, he's already at the Stafford Building."

"At seven in the morning?"

"I've known him to come to work even earlier. There were times when he first took over the company that he worked around the clock."

Erin set her cup down on the coffee table. "Would you tell me which floor he'd be on in the Stafford Building?"

"Of course. I'll also give you a little insight into the mind of Judd Stafford, even though you haven't asked for it. Judd is like the engineer of a locomotive. He pushes the throttle to full speed ahead when he wants something, and keeps on track until he gets it. It's part of his nature. He doesn't stop for anything, even when pausing would save him a lot of time."

"So how do you slow him down when he has a full head of steam?"

"I find ordering him to sit down and shut up usually works." She laughed. "Then again, sometimes it doesn't."

Getting to her feet, Erin held out her hand. "It's been a pleasure to meet you, Miss McDaniels. I'll keep your advice in mind. I have a feeling I'll need all the help I can get in order to get Judd to listen to me."

Fiona walked her to the door. "You'll do just fine. Judd is a very loyal man. He will do anything for the people he loves."

Erin tried to keep Fiona's words in mind as she rode the elevator up to the floor where Judd had his new office. She hesitated when the doors opened, then forced herself to leave the elevator.

There had been times in her life when she'd been extremely nervous, but never like this. But then nothing in her life had ever been as important as Judd.

The door to his office was partially open, and she gave it a little nudge, opening it farther. Judd was sitting behind a large sprawling desk writing on a yellow legal pad. The light from the desk lamp was the only illumination in the room, since the blinds covering the window behind him were still drawn.

As she stood in the doorway watching him, Erin saw him throw his pen down and close his eyes as he leaned back in his chair.

He looked so tired, she thought. His tie had been discarded, and several buttons on his shirt were unfastened. A faint shadow covered the lower half of his jaw, as though he hadn't shaved for a while. His appearance made her believe he hadn't come in early. She had the feeling he'd been there all night.

The energy that usually emanated from him was oddly missing. Had she done that to him? she wondered.

"Judd?"

He opened his eyes and stared at her, his gaze narrowing. "Erin?"

She stepped closer, into the light. "Yes."

He sat forward as though he were going to get up, then settled back in the chair. "What are you doing here?"

Erin's heart felt as though it were permanently lodged in her throat. He didn't sound very glad to see her. Somehow she was going to have to make him change his mind.

She took another step forward. "I want to talk to you."

He wearily rubbed the back of his neck. "We tried that yesterday on the beach. We didn't accomplish much."

"I know. That was my fault. I had been trying to adjust to you being gone, then suddenly you appeared. At first I thought I must be dreaming. By the time I got over the shock of seeing you again, you had gone. You didn't give me a chance to explain."

His mouth twisted with self-mockery. "I've been told I have a habit of doing that."

She walked all the way to his desk. "I heard about some of your bad habits from your secretary."

"Fiona? When did you talk to her?"

"This morning. When I went to the condo."

For a few seconds his gaze searched her face thoroughly. Then he asked, "Why did you go there?"

"To see you."

"Why?"

For an intelligent man, Erin thought with frustration, he was being remarkably obtuse. "To give you another chance."

He made a choking sound that could have been a laugh or a snort of disbelief. Or both. He leaned even farther back in his chair. "Do you really think I deserve another chance?"

This wasn't going at all the way she thought it would. "Do you want one?"

"I asked you first."

"I'm hoping you want another chance," she said as she walked around the desk.

"What I would like," he said, an odd note in his voice, "is for you to tell me what you want from me."

She stopped only inches away from his legs. "I want you to listen to me without interrupting."

"Haven't we done this routine before?"

She wondered if counting to ten would help calm her jangling nerves. Whether it would or not, she didn't take the time to try it. "Fiona said she usually yells at you and makes you sit down so you'll listen to her. You're already sitting down. Do I have to yell at you in order to make you listen to me?"

He shook his head then sat forward and reached for her hand. "Not if you tell me what I want to hear."

She gasped when his grip tightened and he pulled her onto his lap. The feel of his hard thighs beneath hers momentarily distracted her, and she struggled to gather her thoughts. "I know I've been stubborn about trying to do everything my own way in my own time. That wasn't the reason I didn't notify you in San Francisco about Roy and Kate leaving and the cottage being sold. I didn't think I had the right to bother you with any of my problems."

"Because you didn't expect me to come back."

She examined his face closely, surprised by the hurt tone in his voice. She bit her lip, then stopped when he raised his hand to stop her, as he'd done before. The feel of his finger gently stroking her lip had her swallowing with difficulty.

"I wanted you to come back," she said. "I didn't expect you to though."

"That's the part I found hard to accept. After everything between us, you still thought I was only having a fling with you."

"One thing I learned after the car accident is that there are certain things I can't control. Maybe that's why I work so hard trying to make the gallery a success. It's something I can do something about. I couldn't make you stay."

"You didn't even try."

She met his gaze. "I'm trying now."

Something changed in his eyes. "I've listened to every word you said, and I understand. It's just not what I want to hear."

She looked away, her heart clenching painfully. She began to slide off his lap, but he placed his hand on her thigh to stop her.

"Let me go, Judd."

"No."

Hope flickered weakly as she groped for the words she knew he wanted to hear. "Do you want me to apologize?"

He shook his head, his gaze intent on hers. "You said you didn't expect me back, but you wanted me to come back. I want to know why you wanted me to return."

She took a deep, steadying breath. "Because I love you."

His arm tightened around her. "I knew that," he said quietly. "I took it for granted you knew that I loved you too."

She relaxed against him. It was going to be all right now. "How did you know?"

"I'm brilliantly perceptive."

"And modest."

"And I'm the only man you've ever slept with. You aren't the type of woman who would make love with a man if she didn't love him."

She wrapped her arms around his neck. "This could get a little scary when you seem to know me better than I know myself."

He brushed his mouth over hers. "You have the rest of your life to figure it out."

When she was allowed to breathe again, she asked, "Are you really moving your headquarters here?"

He twirled a lock of her soft hair around his finger. "It's an accomplished fact. Justine and her husband left for San Francisco yesterday. She's going to take over the office there while her husband does research for a book on earthquakes. They'll fly back for the wedding, of course."

Just when her heart was beating normally again, she thought with fond exasperation, he would say something to make it skip erratically. "Wedding? Who's getting married?"

"We are."

She leaned away from him so she could stare at him. "Just like that?"

"Well, we'll probably have to suffer through all the various fittings, and my sisters will probably insist on giving you one of those shower things women seem to enjoy before a wedding, but it will be worth it in the end. Then there's always your brothers . . ."

She shifted on his lap. "What about my brothers?"

He held her still. "I don't think you should be squirming like that under the circumstances, sweetheart. We're having a serious discussion here."

"About a wedding."

"Our wedding," he said with a hint of smugness. "Michael has given his consent and approval. All he needs is the date so he can give you away."

She blinked. "Why does Michael know about our wedding, and I've only just heard about it?"

Judd's smile was relaxed; his eyes were glowing with love. "That's where I made a mistake. I took it for granted you already knew we were a permanent arrangement. I told Michael he didn't have to worry about you any longer because I was going to make sure you would be the happiest woman in Hawaii."

She shook her head. "What am I going to tell our children when they want to know where we were when you proposed?"

"You can tell them you were sitting on my lap in my office." He brought her closer, his arms tightening possessively around her. "However," he added, his lips against hers, "you don't need to tell them what followed my proposal."

Smiling, Erin gave herself over to the glory of being in his arms. Forever.

# THE EDITOR'S CORNER

Next month LOVESWEPT celebrates heroes, those irresistible men who sweep us off our feet, who tantalize us with whispered endearments, and who challenge us with their teasing humor and hidden vulnerability. Whether they're sexy roughnecks or dashing sophisticates, dark and dangerous or blond and brash, these men are heartthrobs, the kind no woman can get enough of. And you can feast your eyes on six of them as they alone grace each of our truly special covers next month. HEARTTHROBS—heroes who'll leave you spellbound as only real men can.

Who better to lead our HEARTTHROBS lineup than Fayrene Preston and her hero, Max Hayden, in **A MAGNIFICENT AFFAIR**, LOVESWEPT #528? Max is the best kind of kisser: a man who takes his time and takes a woman's breath away. And when Ashley Whitfield crashes her car into his seaside inn, he senses she's one sweet temptation he could go on kissing forever. But Ashley has made a habit of drifting through her life, and it'll take all of Max's best moves to keep her in his arms for good. A magnificent love story, by one of the best in the genre.

The utterly delightful **CALL ME SIN**, LOVESWEPT #529, by award-winner Jan Hudson, will have you going wild over Ross Berringer, a Texas Ranger as long and as tall as his twin brother, Holt, who thrilled readers in **BIG AND BRIGHT**, LOVESWEPT #464. The fun in **CALL ME SIN** begins when handsome hunk Ross moves in next door to Susan Sinclair. He's the excitement the prim bookstore owner has been missing in her life—and the perfect partner to help her track down a con artist. But once Ross's downright neighborly attention turns Susan inside out with ecstasy, she starts running scared. How Ross unravels her intriguing mix of passion and fear is a sinfully delicious story you'll want to read.

Doris Parmett outdoes herself in creating a perfect HEARTTHROB in **MR. PERFECT**, LOVESWEPT #530. Chase Rayburn is the epitome of sex appeal, a confirmed bachelor who can charm a lady's socks off—and then all the rest of her clothes. So why does he feel wildly jealous over Sloan McKay's personal ad on a billboard? He's always been close to his law partner's widow and young son, but he's never before wanted to kiss Sloan until she melted with wanton pleasure. Shocking desire, daring seduction, and a friendship that deepens into love—a breathtaking combination in one terrific book.

Dangerously sexy, his gaze full of delicious promises, Hunter Kincaid will have you dreaming of **LOVE AND A BLUE-EYED COWBOY**, LOVESWEPT #531, by Sandra Chastain. Hunter knows he can win the top prize in a motorcycle scavenger hunt, but he doesn't count on being partnered with petite, smart-mouthed Fortune Dagosta. A past sorrow has hardened Hunter's heart, and the last person he wants for a companion for a week is a beautiful woman whose compassion is easily aroused and whose body is made for loving. Humorous and poignant, the sensual adventure that follows is a real winner!

Imagine a man who has muscles like boulders and a smoky drawl that conjures up images of rumpled sheets and long, deep kisses—that's Storm Dalton, Tami Hoag's hero in **TAKEN BY STORM**, LOVESWEPT #532. A man like that gets what he wants, and what he wants is Julia McCarver. But he's broken her heart more than once, and she has no intention of giving him another chance. Years of being a winning quarterback has taught Storm ways to claim victory, and the way he courts Julia is a thrilling and funny romance that'll keep you turning the pages.

Please give a rousing welcome to new author Linda Warren and her first LOVESWEPT, **BRANDED**, #532, a vibrantly emotional romance that has for a hero one of the most virile rodeo cowboys ever. Tanner Danielson has one rule in life: Never touch another man's wife. And though he wanted Julie Fielding from the first time he saw her, he never tasted her fire because she belonged to another. But now she's free and he isn't waiting a moment longer. A breathlessly exciting love story with all the wonderfully evocative writing that Linda displayed in her previous romances.

On sale this month from FANFARE are three marvelous novels. **LIGHTS ALONG THE SHORE**, by immensely talented first-time author Diane Austell, is set in nineteenth-century California, and as the dramatic events of that fascinating period unfold, beautiful, impetuous Marin Gentry must face up to the challenges in her turbulent life, including tangling with notorious Vail Severance. Highly acclaimed Patricia Potter delivers **LAWLESS**, a poignant historical romance about a schoolteacher who longs for passionate love and finds her dreams answered by a coldhearted gunfighter who's been hired to drive her off her land. In **HIGHLAND REBEL**, beloved author Stephanie Bartlett whisks you away to the rolling hills and misty valleys of the Isle of Skye, where proud highland beauty Catriona Galbraith is fighting for her land and her people, and where bold Texas rancher Ian MacLeod has sworn to win her love.

Also available this month in the hardcover edition from Doubleday (and in paperback from FANFARE in March) is **LUCKY'S LADY** by ever-popular LOVESWEPT author Tami Hoag. Those of you who were enthralled with the Cajun rogue Remy Doucet in **THE RESTLESS HEART**, LOVESWEPT #458, will find yourself saying Ooh la la when you meet his brother, Lucky, for he is one rough and rugged man of the bayou. And when he takes the elegent Serena Sheridan through a Louisiana swamp to find her grandfather, they generate what *Romantic Times* has described as "enough steam heat to fog up any reader's glasses."

Happy reading!

With warmest wishes,

*Nita Taublib*

Nita Taublib
Associate Publisher/LOVESWEPT
Publishing Associate/FANFARE

Don't miss these fabulous Bantam Fanfare titles
on sale in JANUARY.

## LIGHTS ALONG THE SHORE
by Diane Austell

## LAWLESS
by Pat Potter

## HIGHLAND REBEL
by Stephanie Bartlett

**Ask for them by name.**

## LIGHTS ALONG THE SHORE

### BY DIANE AUSTELL

The Gentrys. They had left the comforts of the Old South and come to California, a sunlit Eden where ranchers put down roots and grew wealthy, while beautiful young women such as Marin Gentry danced until dawn and dreamed of undying love. But ahead was turmoil no man or woman could foresee: the discovery of gold, with its lure of easy money and easier death, the dizzying growth of bawdy San Francisco, the gathering stormclouds of Civil War. . . .

\*      \*      \*

Marin Severance is reunited with her brother-in-law, Vail, for the first time since the night, several years before, when she was still unmarried, and he seduced her. . . .

Stuart had gone to San Francisco four days ago to buy parts for the water pump, and she expected him home for supper.

There were sounds of horses pounding past the side of the house and Stuart's voice calling to Mateo. Then boots on the wooden floor of the back porch and the kitchen door banging open. Marin swung around with flour still on her hands and a smile of greeting on her face. Coming in the door were Stuart, Michael, and, just behind them, Vail Severance.

She picked up a towel, wiped her hands, and moved to Stuart for a kiss of welcome. She said something to Michael, although she couldn't hear her own voice for the roaring in her ears.

What could she do? Where could she look? She must speak to him, look at him, smile at him. It would seem very odd if she didn't. But all the blood in her body seemed to have rushed into her head. Oh, God, how could she explain to Stuart why the sight of his brother upset her so? She forced herself to look into Vail's eyes, and the buzzing in her head made her think she was going to faint.

There was nothing at all in those clear gray eyes but friendliness and the mildest sort of interest, the kind of interest a man might show on greeting his brother's wife, a girl he had known slightly at some time in the distant past. She put out her hand because she had to, felt the corners of her mouth go up in a smile, and heard him say, "Hello, Red."

Somewhere she found the strength to say, "Welcome, Vail. Have you come home to stay?"

Supper went off smoothly, and by the time Luz served the cobbler and cream, Marin had decided that she was going to live after all. Stuart appeared to have noticed nothing odd about her behavior, perhaps because he had been pulling off his coat when she spoke to Vail and had his back turned. Michael had simply stood there and smiled as he always did when he saw her, and as for Vail—Papa and Ethan had clearly been right about the memory-destroying properties of alcohol, for he obviously recalled nothing about that night. He treated her just as he always had, perhaps a little more courteously because of her increased age and status, but that was all. . . .

After supper Marin sat down by the parlor fire in her favorite chair, the one Rose had used in the old days, and picked up a shirt of Stuart's to mend, thinking with relief that she now had a little time to compose herself. She looked up, and the thread snapped in her fingers. Vail had come into the room alone.

Damn the man! Why couldn't he go look at the horse or the pump, or tend to some other masculine matter? Why did he have to follow her in here, where there was no one else to share the burden of conversation? The business of rethreading the needle took her close attention, but she watched him covertly, noticing the way he moved, the vitality in his face.

He sat down opposite her and stretched his booted legs toward the flames, and she busied herself with the torn frill of Stuart's shirt, wondering how long she could maintain this domestic pose and make some kind of polite conversation.

Her mind fumbled, searching for something to say, and Petra came in with her gliding, boneless walk. She set the tray bearing coffeepot and cups on the table next to Marin and, as she bent forward, murmured, "Carey is still awake, Miss Marin. Should I bring him down?"

Marin snatched at the suggestion like a drowning man at a straw. Young as he was, Carey, had a gift for drawing all eyes to him—in this case, away from her.

"Yes, bring him down," she said gratefully.

"How is my mother?" Vail asked suddenly. He was lighting a cigar and frowning into the fire.

It was a safe subject. "Not well," Marin answered, her eyes on her sewing. "Will you see her before you leave?"

"I can't."

She looked up, thinking of Ethan. It was such a sorry, stupid situation. "Surely your father wouldn't object? She's quite ill, I think."

"He would object—which would make it worse for her." A smile crossed his face, and Marin caught her breath at the bitterness in it. Without watching her hand, she shoved the needle through the cloth and jabbed her finger. A bright drop of blood appeared, and she scowled and put it to her mouth.

Vail's smile became genuine. "You looked like a child when you did that. I keep forgetting how young you are."

It was the first personal remark he'd made, and it unnerved her so much that she almost dropped the shirt. He must not have noticed though, for he went right on, "This is the first chance I've had to apologize for my conduct the night of Celia's party. I was very rude."

The finger remained in her mouth; her heart seemed to come to a standstill. He did remember, then, and he was apologizing for *rudeness*?

She was not thinking clearly, but she heard him say, "I had a bad case of hurt feelings that night, as you probably know, and I'm sorry to say I got very drunk. I seem to remember leaving you on the dance floor with Gerald Crown, which I certainly would never have done in my right mind. I hope you've forgiven me."

Her heart began to beat again. He thought he'd left her with Gerald.

"Oh, I forgave you immediately. Gerald is charming and a very good dancer." She picked up the coffeepot and began to pour with a steady hand.

He winced. "I deserved that. My brother married a quick-witted lady as well as a beautiful one. I wasn't so lucky."

He was thinking of Celia. Should she mention her? No, better not. Petra brought in Carey, and Marin took him on her lap with relief. Vail leaned forward and looked him over.

"A handsome boy," he said finally.

She warmed to the praise, as she always did to any kind words for Carey.

"Yes," she said, and laughed. "Forgive me, I can't be modest. I think he's handsome, too." She set the child on the floor, and he immediately went up on all fours and started to rock so vigorously that he tumbled over and lay there crowing. Then he struggled up and tried again to move forward.

Vail took his cup, watching with a smile.

"I suppose Father is delighted."

"Oh, yes. He was miffed at first when we didn't name the

baby after him, but he got over it when he decided that Carey looked like him. At present he's very pleased with me."

"And with Stuart, too, I imagine. Well, Stuart always had the knack of pleasing him. I never did." He said it without self-pity, but Marin remembered Celia's words: "His father hurt him badly."

She picked up her own cup. "Except for your mother, no one agrees with him. My mother thinks Carey strongly resembles her family, the Landrinis, and my father says he looks like me."

Carey raised his head as if he knew he was being discussed, and Vail watched him, moved—even more than he had expected—by emotions hard to analyze. Shame at what he had done to this girl, so innocent and so drunk—it had all been his fault. Respect for her cool courage when she first saw him in the kitchen and her poker player's skill when she showed him her baby. Surprising sadness at the knowledge that, for the baby's sake and for hers, he could never claim the boy as his own. Wonder at the simple fact of the child. There might be other children in the world who were his, but none he knew of, none so certain as this little boy looking up at him with great black eyes shining.

He said, "Your father is right. At least he has his mother's wonderful eyes."

Carey spared her the necessity of a reply. He made a tremendous effort, lifted one tiny hand, brought it forward, and moved the knee behind it. Then he moved the other hand and knee, lifted his head, and chortled.

"Oh!" Marin breathed. "He's done it, he's crawling. Oh, he's been trying so hard!"

Carey began to move faster and faster now that he had figured out the difficult business, traveling in a circle with a triumphant gurgling laugh until he fell in a heap at Vail's feet. Immediately he got up and sat down again with a plop. The man above him extended a finger for him to tug, and the child examined it interestedly, talking to himself in a cooing babble.

Vail looked down at the soft, dark curls. "So now I am an uncle. God, it makes me feel old."

"Ethan is an uncle, too, but he doesn't know it."

"No word at all?"

"Nothing. I think about the knife fights and the hangings in the gold camps. Sometimes I'm afraid . . ."

"Don't be. Ethan can take care of himself. He's a good man in a fight, but he doesn't look for trouble."

"It need never have happened. Papa will never be well, and Mama—she is not herself at all. It was all so stupid . . ."

"Tragedies usually are, because people are stupid. I'm in the camps fairly often. I have business there at times. Ever since I heard about Ethan, I've kept an eye out for him, and I'll continue to."

With a rush of gratitude she said, "Oh, it would mean so much just to know that he's alive, even if he doesn't come home." Impulsively she added, "It's a shame Logan didn't know you were coming. Next time let us know, and I'll make sure she's here."

Why had she said that? Only minutes before she had been hoping never to see this man again, and now she had invited him to come back and to meet Logan in her home, which would make an enemy of Malcolm if he found out. No help for it now. She couldn't take back the invitation, not with him smiling at her like that and the warm light again in his eyes.

"That's very kind. I worry about Logan, trapped in that house."

"There's no place else she'd want to be, not now, with her mother sick. But—do come back. Seeing you will help her, I'm sure of that."

# LAWLESS

## BY PATRICIA POTTER

### Author of RAINBOW

"One of the romance genre's finest talents . . ."
—*Romantic Times*

IN LAWLESS, Patricia Potter tells the dramatic and compelling story of a brave schoolteacher and the lawless outcast who becomes her protector. When Willow Taylor refuses to sell her land to powerful rancher Alex Newton, legendary gunfighter Lobo is hired to drive her away. But his attempts go awry as he ends up rescuing members of her "family" from disasters, including a fire. Worse, he's shocked to discover that Willow is unlike the heartless women he's known only too well. As more gunslingers arrive, wreaking havoc in a once peaceful community, Willow remains undaunted, and Lobo feels the heat of unbidden longing for this strong and beautiful survivor.

In the following excerpt, Lobo has broken off with Newton and has temporarily sided with Willow. Under a velvet-dark sky, he finds himself opening up to her as he never had with anyone before. . . .

\*      \*      \*

"Why do they call you Lobo?"

He shrugged. "The Apache gave me the name. It seemed as good as any."

"As good as Jess," she asked, using his real name.

He scowled. "I told you he died."

Willow didn't say anything, but the silence was heavy with her doubt.

He turned away from her. "Lobo fits, lady. Believe me."

"The wolf is a social animal," Willow said as if reading out of a book. "He mates for life."

Lobo turned and stared at her icily. "Unless he's an outcast, chased from the pack, and then he turns on his own kind." There was no self-pity in the observation, only the cold recital of fact.

"Is that what happened?"

Lobo felt his gut wrench. He'd never meant to say what he had, had not even consciously thought it before. A cold dread seeped through him as he realized how much control of himself he was losing.

"Lady, I've done things that would make you puke. So why don't you go back to your nice little house and leave me alone."

Willow hesitated. She sensed the turmoil in him, and it echoed her own churning emotions.

"I don't care about the past," she finally said.

He laughed roughly. "I don't scare you at all?"

She knew he wanted her to say yes. She knew she should say yes. She should be fearful of someone with his reputation, his life. But she wasn't.

"No," she answered.

"You don't know me, lady."

"Willow."

He shook his head. "And the last thing you should do is be out here with me."

"Were you with the Apache long?" she asked softly.

It was a sneaky question, and he stiffened. "Long enough."

She sensed his withdrawal, if it was possible that he could distance himself any farther than he already had. The kiss might never have happened, except it was so vivid in her mind.

Her hand went out to his, which was wrapped around the post. "Thank you for staying."

His hand seemed to tremble, and she wondered if she imagined it.

"You may not be grateful long," he replied shortly.

"You will stay, then?"

"A few days," he replied. "But the town won't like it. I'm usually not welcome."

"If Alex can hire you, I can," she answered defiantly.

"But Newton has money, and you . . . ?"

Again the implication was clear, and she knew she was flushing a bright red. She hoped the moonlight didn't reveal it, but she saw the glint in his eye and knew her hope was in vain.

Her thoughts turned to what had been nagging her, to the violent death that had occurred just hours earlier. "You won't have to fight Marsh Canton if you stay?" Her hand shook slightly as she posed the haunting question.

The glint was still in his eye. "A lot of folks been waiting for that."

"I've never seen anyone so . . . fast," she whispered.

His right hand went to his neck. "He's good. Aren't you going to ask me if I'm just as good?"

She didn't want to think of him that way. She preferred thinking of him hauling her poor bull Jupiter from the burning barn. "No," she whispered.

"That's what I do, you know," he persisted almost angrily. "I'm no hero like you want to believe. I'm a killer just like Canton. You want to know how many people I've killed?"

Her gaze was glued to his eyes, to the swirling, dangerous currents in them. She heard the raw self-contempt in his voice, but what he was saying didn't matter to her, not to the way she felt about him, not to the way she wanted to . . . touch and hold and . . .

"I was twelve when I first killed," he continued in the same voice. "Twelve. I found I was real good at it."

His eyes, filled with tormented memories and even rage, blazed directly at her. And she felt her need for him deepen, felt her heart pound with the compulsion to disprove his reason for self-derision.

But she couldn't move, and she had no words that wouldn't anger or hurt or sound naive and silly. That, she sensed, was what he was waiting for so he could have a reason to leave. The currents running between them were stronger than ever, and Lobo was willing her to say or do something to destroy it, but she was just as determined not to. Silence stretched between but something else too, something so strong that neither could back away.

If she'd offered compassion or sympathy, Lobo could have

broken through her hold on him. But she gave neither. Instead, he was warmed by the unfamiliar glow of understanding, of unquestioning acceptance. He basked in it, feeling whole for the first time that he could remember. All of a sudden he realized this was what he'd been searching for, not freedom but something so elusive he'd never been able to put a name to it.

And it was too late. His insides churned and twisted with pure agony as he realized that one indisputable fact. He carried too much trouble with him. His reputation, which he had so carefully nurtured, was a noose around his neck. The older he got, the more the rope tightened. He could live with that, but he couldn't live with the fact that it was also a noose around the neck of anyone foolish enough to care for him.

He forced himself to take a step back, to fight his way out of the moment's intimacy, one deeper than any he'd ever shared with a person, deeper than when he plunged his manhood into a woman. Christ!

"Lady, you should run like hell!" His voice was harsh, grating. "You and those kids don't need the kind of grief I bring."

She worried her lips as she sought for something to say, to somehow express her belief in him, but before she found the words, he spoke again.

"And I sure as hell don't need *you*." He emphasized the last word as if trying to convince himself, and once again he stepped back.

"Jess . . ."

His mouth seemed to soften for a moment, and he hesitated. But then his mouth firmed again, and his eyes turned hard. He bowed slightly, mockingly. "If I'm going to be of any use to you, ma'am, I'd better turn in."

He strolled lazily back to the barn and disappeared within, leaving Willow feeling desolate and alone.

# HIGHLAND REBEL

## BY STEPHANIE BARTLETT

## Author of HIGHLAND JADE

Catriona Galbraith was a proud highland beauty who would do anything to stop a tyranical laird from possessing her homeland and heritage. Ian McLeod was the bold Texas rancher who swore to win Cat's love from the moment he laid eyes on the bewitching young woman. But Ian didn't know the dangerous secret that beckoned to Cat night after night: a secret that could sow the seeds of rebellion and destroy their passion.

\*      \*      \*

Squares of yellow lamplight stained the snow in front of the church. Ian pulled his muffler tight against an icy gust as he followed Colin up the stone steps. The wind grew even colder after the winter sun went down.

Warm air, thick with the smells of wool and sweat, surrounded Ian as he sidled through the door. The interior droned with excited voices, all talking at once. Small wonder after the last two days.

Mindful of his height, he settled himself in the back pew. Colin patted his shoulder, then moved on up the aisle toward the front, where he could see and hear. For once Ian was glad to be an outlander. Without the old man around, the other crofters still ignored him for the most part, and that was fine with him. He didn't much want to talk to anybody anyhow. All they wanted to do was crow about their victories over the sheriff's men.

He wondered whatever had possessed the courts to send another officer the next day, trying to serve papers of some kind. Fin Lewis made short work of the man, a kid really. Tossed his papers in the muddy snow and escorted him to the edge of the estate at the point of his pike.

Ian rubbed at a smudge of soot staining his fingers. Most of the crofters wanted justice for themselves, but Fin liked to fight, bullying men who were outnumbered a hundred to one. Granddaddy always said there was one in every bunch.

He shrugged. At least they were on the same side, although he'd wager Fin was only concerned for himself. He didn't like the fella, didn't trust him at all. He only hoped he wouldn't ever have to depend on him.

Damn! The last thing he wanted to think about tonight was Lewis. Crossing his arms over his chest, he glanced around the room. The stone building was packed, every pew full to overflowing with men. Many of them even brought their families.

Gavin Nicolson smiled and waved from a few rows up. The man nudged the woman beside him. His daughter Belag. She turned and smiled back over her shoulder, but her cheeks crimsoned and she turned away when he tipped his hat. A pretty little thing with brown hair and dark eyes. She'd make some man a fine wife.

He tried to image himself with her, then shook his head to clear it. He knew he'd never love another woman, Catriona owned his heart, and she always would. Maybe someday his memories would dim enough so he could marry and have a family. But he didn't hold out much hope.

If only he could see Cat again, just for one night. He ached to put his arms around her, hold her, make love to her. His lips twisted into a bitter smile. She didn't love him, didn't want him, or she would have agreed to marry him. No, he might as well wish for a magic pony to ride him home to Texas across the clouds.

He wondered how things were at the Braes, with the poor crops and the hard winter. He missed Fergus and Jennet, Effie would be growing, and Geordie must be almost a man. It would be spring again soon. Two years since Granddaddy died. Two years since he met Catriona in the graveyard. Would his life ever be right again?

The voices around him subsided, bringing him out of his reverie. Dugald Purcell mounted the steps and took his place in the pulpit. "My friends, we have faced the enemy, and we have won!" A cheer echoed back from the rafters. Purcell went on, but Ian listened with only half an ear.

He shifted on the hard seat, trying to think how to go about settling these folks down. He could understand them being happy about running the sheriff out of town, but he figured they didn't know how dangerous it was to fight the law. And a lot of good it did him to warn Purcell, telling him what Campbell had said about the army; he just nodded and said, "Aye." And now he'd called another meeting.

A second figure moved up the pulpit steps, a woman, her head shrouded with a tartan shawl. Ian leaned forward. He'd seen her somewhere before. The image flashed through his mind, the woman who spoke with Purcell just before the fight at the bridge.

He caught the last of Purcell's words, something about a visitor who wanted to help plan their next actions. The slender figure stood beside the crofter. Facing the crowd, she lifted the shawl from her head, letting it drop to her shoulders. Black curls cascaded over her shoulders, and even from the back of the church, Ian could see her eyes were a deep blue. But it wasn't until she smiled that he knew for sure.

Catriona.

Catriona lay back on the musty coverlet and closed her eyes. Weariness weighed on her, the tension of the last few days and nights aching in every muscle. She was grateful for a bed and a room where she could be alone. On the edge of sleep, Ian's face floated before her.

Her body throbbed a bittersweet tune. She'd hungered for the sight of him for months, months with no word even to say he was still alive, still on Skye. Then tonight, as they ushered her into a church full of nervous crofters, there he stood.

She gave the speech Hugh helped her write before she left the Braes, rallying them to the cause and answering their questions. But she never forgot for a moment that he was there, sitting in the back, head and shoulders taller than the men around him. She tried not to look, but she couldn't keep her eyes away from him. The way his fine blond hair strayed across his forehead, shining in the lamplight, the way his handsome face eased into a smile and his eyes never strayed from her face as she talked. When the meeting ended and the crofters poured out the tall doors, she looked for him, but he'd vanished.

Cat rolled over and punched a hollow in the hard pillow. If only they could talk. Now, with them both fighting the lairds, he had to understand why she couldn't marry him and go to America, why she had to stay on Skye.

She tossed onto her back and stared up at the rafters. Tomorrow she'd find him, go to the forge and talk to him, tell him how much she missed him, how much she loved him. A smile curved her lips and she closed her eyes. Everything would be the way it was last spring.

A soft tapping startled her from a near-dream. It was late. Most of the guests at the lodge were asleep. She slid off the narrow bed and crept to the door, keeping her feet silent and her voice low. "Who is it?"

"Ian. Let me in."

Her pulse raced and she could scarcely catch her breath as she undid the bolt and pulled him into the room. In one move her arms went around his neck and her lips pressed his. Ian's love surrounded her, his hands traveling over her body. A delicious warmth swirled in her head and down her spine to end pulsing low in her belly.

Then Ian's hands cupped her shoulders and pushed her down onto the bed. She lay back and held up her arms to receive him.

He stood beside the bed, frowning down at her. "Cat, how can you do this?"

She sat up, her face flushed with disappointment and confusion. "Do what?"

"Risk your life traveling the countryside, stirring up trouble. Fighting the constables. I saw you in the crowd the other day. And the march to Dunvegan tomorrow. What will happen if you get caught?"

Anger kindled from the ashes of her longing. "Why, the same that'll happen if they catch you, I suppose."

His mouth opened, then snapped shut. "You don't

understand. The sergeant we chased out of here yesterday said the sheriff has asked for the army to come in."

The army. Purcell hadn't mentioned it. She bit her lip, trying to keep from shivering. "I hope they do," her voice sounded stronger than she felt.

He stared at her, his eyes wide. "A real war. Is that what you want?"

She tossed her head. "The eyes of the country are on Skye. The public is with us now. If they send the army against us, it can only make our case stronger."

He tossed up his hands and paced across the threadbare carpet. "And if they shoot people, will it be worth it then? Do you want to die?"

Cat swallowed before she answered. "Do you?" Her voice sounded hollow in her ears. She knew she didn't want to die, nor did she want him to die. Would the army really shoot to kill?

He stopped pacing and turned to face her, holding his clenched fists at his sides. "It's not the same thing. I'm a man."

"I've not forgotten what you are, but I see no difference in the risks we take." She pushed herself to her feet. "And you, what reason have you to fight the lairds? You're not even a proper Scotsman."

His full lips thinned to a hard line. "I'm a Macleod, same as the landlord. It's my duty to help make things right."

She took a step closer and planted her hands on her hips. "Aye, and I'm a Galbraith and a Macdonald. And I was born and bred a crofter, not a rich landowner from America."

The heat of his body reached out to her, but she fought the urge to touch him. Weariness settled over her again, and she looked away. It was no use—he'd never understand. "I've no more to say to you, so I'll thank you to leave now." She turned her back to him.

"Cat." His voice caressed her, and the longing pulsed deep in her belly. His hands slid down her shoulders and turned her toward him. Without a word he drew her into his arms and kissed her deep and long. Cat melted against him.

His mouth still clinging to hers, he lifted her and carried her to the bed.

She lay back, savoring the sweetness of his mouth on hers, the weight of his body pressing against her. His fingers fumbled at the buttons of her blouse, and then his hand cupped her breast, the work-roughened palm brushing her nipple. She gasped with pleasure as his lips followed his hand.

She traced the planes of his muscles, trailing her fingers down his chest. Trembling, she unfastened his trousers, slid her hands inside, and caressed the feverish hardness of his body.

He moaned and kissed her, pressing his lips against her mouth, her eyelids, her throat. His hands slid beneath her skirt, bunching the hem up around her waist. When his fingers smoothed the length of her thighs, caressing her secret pleasure, she arched against him in a fever of desire.

Unable to wait any longer, she tugged his trousers down over his buttocks and guided him inside her, closing her eyes and moaning as he filled her. She rose to meet him, wave after wave of pleasure washing through her, until she cried out, spilling over with delicious agony. Somewhere above her she heard him moan, and felt him collapse on top of her.

Without opening her eyes she slid her arms around him, holding his body against her. *Ian*. His name danced through her mind, making its own melody of love. Nothing else mattered.

# FANFARE

## On Sale in February

*New York Times* Bestseller

# TEXAS! SAGE

☐ (29500-4) $4.99/5.99 in Canada
### by Sandra Brown

*The third and final book in Sandra Brown's beloved TEXAS! trilogy.
Sage Tyler always thought she wanted a predictable, safe man . . . until a
lean, blue-eyed drifter took her breath, and then her heart away.*

# SONG OF THE WOLF

☐ (29014-2) $4.99?5.99 in Canada
### by Rosanne Bittner

*Young, proud, and beautiful, Medicine Wolf possesses extraordinary
healing powers and a unique sensitivity that leads her on an unforgettable
odyssey into a primeval world of wildness, mystery, and passion.*

# LATE NIGHT DANCING

☐ (29557-8) $5.99/6.99 in Canada
### by Diana Silber

*A compelling novel of three friends -- sophisticated Los Angeles women with
busy, purposeful lives, who also live on the fast track of romance and sex,
because, like lonely women everywhere, they hunger for a man to love.*

# SUMMER'S KNIGHT

☐ (29549-7) $4.50/5.50 in Canada
### by Virginia Lynn

*Heiress Summer St. Clair is stranded penniless on the streets of London.
But her terrifying ordeal soon turns to adventure when she captures the
glittering eyes of the daring Highland rogue, Jamie Cameron.*

☐ Please send me the books I have checked above. I am enclosing $ _____ (add $2.50 to cover
postage and handling).  Send check or money order, no cash or C. O. D.'s please.

Mr./ Ms. _____

Address _____

City/ State/ Zip _____

Send order to: Bantam Books, Dept. FN, 414 East Golf Road, Des Plaines, IL  60016

Please allow four to six weeks for delivery.

Prices and availability subject to change without notice.

## THE SYMBOL OF GREAT WOMEN'S
## FICTION FROM BANTAM

Ask for these books at your local bookstore or use this page to order.

FN23 - 2/92